CASUAL MAGIC

Dan Ackerman

Supposed Crimes LLC • Matthews, North Carolina

For David

IT HAD been dark, just before dawn, when West had left the house for the jog. He tried to go every morning, with a lot of emphasis on tried, but it wasn't his fault that it had been bitterly cold and snowy all winter. Spring had started to show its face and West had vowed to get back into a routine. He would be good, watch what he ate, and shed those ten pounds of winter weight. Maybe he would let Laurel set him up on a date. Maybe.

A date could be fun. It had been a long time since he'd been on a date and longer since he'd had fun on one, but he felt like it was time to get back in the game. Even if he didn't find that swooning, immediate love of myth, maybe he'd at least get laid. It had been a long time since he'd gotten that. Long enough that he refused to answer when his friends asked.

As he approached the house, his hopeful mood soured as the light of day revealed a man sitting on his front steps.

Not just any man, but a light-skinned man in his early thirties that absolutely screamed trouble, from his ripped black jeans and scuffed boots to the cigarette that dangled between his fingers. He had his eyes fixed on the cigarette, not really smoking, just watching it go to ash. He glanced up when West got a little closer to the house, took a drag, then stubbed out the cigarette. He stood and moved towards West.

"I, uh." The man raked a hand through his perfectly not-perfect hair, messy and unkempt, but not dirty looking. "Are you Wesley Archer?"

"Westley," West corrected reflexively.

The man nodded and opened his mouth.

West pointed to the cigarette butt that he'd left on the walkway. "You're not planning on leaving that there."

"Oh. No." He picked it up and glanced around. His eyes settled on the garbage can by the garage and he flicked it in, his aim uncommonly good.

Not surprising, West decided. The man had the look of a demon, with plenty of human dilution, of course, but not too many people had red eyes unless they had the Devil for an ancestor. The dark brick, more brown than red, of the man's eyes told West all he needed to know about him.

West walked past the man and got up two steps before the man said, "You're supposed to be able to answer questions."

"Anyone can answer questions." It was his usual brush off. It kept away those who had only hearsay to go on. People who had no business coming tracking him down to where he lived and asking him all sorts of things and bringing trouble around with them. The neighbors had noticed and brought it up to Laurel; that had been a mess to talk his way out of.

The man shoved his hand into the pocket of his leather jacket and rummaged for so long that West had almost reached the front door by the time he produced a black coin. He held it out to West uncertainly, this movement sending along the smell of cigarettes and old-fashioned cologne.

West eyed the coin, then took it with a sigh. The black wood was well-worn, and the symbol etched on one side had almost been rubbed off altogether. He squinted at it, making sure it was the right symbol. A few people had tried to hand him knock-offs and he'd been more careful since he'd gotten fooled by one.

"Fine."

"Do you think I could come in?" The man glanced up and down the street, his eyes skating over the cookie-cutter houses, the endless SUVs, the clean and straight sidewalks without any cracks. "It's sort of sensitive, what I need to ask about?"

He handed back the coin. "Come back later."

The man's eyebrows, dark and angular, shot up. "Sorry?"

"Come back later. I just ran five miles and I need to get to work."

"Oh." The man scrubbed a hand over the faint stubble on his face. "Are you sure we can't talk about this now?"

"Very."

West, in fact, did not have to go to work. He hadn't had a steady job in a while, instead subsisting on witchy odd jobs advertised in the *Daily Craft* and whatever else he could pick up. Random strangers hunting him down to answer questions didn't pay and it had been made clear to him that he wasn't allowed to charge for it, at least, not in a currency he could use.

No, this was his end of the bargain he'd made at the clearly very wise and informed age of thirteen. Not too many people had come around lately and he'd hoped that he'd gotten a reputation as surly and less than helpful. He hated their weird questions and hated the reminder that he'd basically sold his soul for a guy who hadn't even known his name.

"When should I come back?" the demon asked.

"Around lunchtime, I guess."

West left him out there, felt almost bad for about half a second before he remembered that he didn't owe this guy anything, that the only reason he ever had to deal with these people was because of stupid Jeremey Nivens.

Jeremey Nivens and his torn rotator cuff.

Jeremey Nivens and his gorgeous body, and his picture-perfect face and his smile that had made thirteen-year-old West feel like he could float all the way up to the clouds. He'd been the star player on the school's team and West had avidly entertained the idea that, once West was in high school and Jeremey was a senior, they'd finally see each other enough that Jeremey would realize he liked West just as much as West liked him.

When Jeremey had torn his rotator cuff the summer before West was due to start high school, his chances at a scholarship, at the Minor Leagues and maybe even the Majors, if he really stuck with it, had been blown. And if Jeremey wasn't going to be the star player, then West could never be the star player's boyfriend.

So, infatuated so badly he had fuzz in his head instead of brains, he'd gone through his grandmother's grimoire and found the right spell to conjure the Devil. He'd made the deal with the lanky, monstrous thing that had been the Devil.

Jeremey played for the Mets now.

And every time he ran into West he called him 'Jess.'

West doubled back and made sure the front door was locked before he got in the shower, not wanting to take any risks and find out if that guy was as much trouble as his leather jacket and heavily tattooed hands suggested.

In the shower, West pinched himself, mostly at that extra layer around his belly. When got out of the shower and joined Laurel for breakfast, he eyed her bowl of syrup-laden oatmeal and then his carefully portioned breakfast of cantaloupe (eight ounces) and plain, non-fat Greek yogurt (also eight ounces).

He called himself fat.

Laurel cackled and told him, "Sure! For a gay guy!" and then she poked him in the ribs. "You should let me set you up on a date."

"I've got to lose ten pounds."

"You said that five pounds ago. Come on, there's plenty of girls that would like you."

"I don't know." He didn't know what kind of women Laurel would find for him. He was known to just about everyone in the town of Devonport as Laurel Archer's Gay Brother and had been since sixth grade.

"Women are easier to please. We're not looking for the perfect man with the perfect body and the perfect job and the perfect dick. We're just looking for—"

"Anything with a pulse and modicum of hygiene."

She scowled at him and took a bite of her oatmeal.

The heady, rich smell of real maple syrup, the kind that came from Vermont in glass bottles, tickled his nose. It made his cantaloupe a lot less appetizing. He'd have to start eating breakfast after she left.

"Come on, West. You're a catch," Laurel promised.

"Maybe. I don't know."

He thought of the last online profile he'd bothered to look at. *No fats, no femmes, no Asians.* West was not exactly fat, not exactly femme, and had no idea if he was Asian or not. His mother wasn't exactly sure either. She guessed that his dad might have been "Chinese, or something over there, or maybe Hispanic."

Either way, the combination of his bronze skin, mono-lidded eyes, and wavy hair made people, strangers and acquaintances alike, try to guess where he was from and ask him where he had learned English so well.

Laurel pushed her half-eaten oatmeal towards him. "I'm not going to finish this."

He maintained control.

"Come on, West, eat. You're skinny."

He shrugged.

She put her hand, pale and freckled, over his. "I'm kind of getting worried, you know." She tightened her grip. "So is Mom."

The fact that his mother and sister had been discussing his weight didn't bode well. "I'm just trying to get back to my summer weight. That's it."

"Promise?"

He sighed and twisted his hand so he could grip hers. "I promise." Summer had been the last time he'd felt like anyone would want to see him naked and his preferred way to go on a date was feeling like he could stand to be seen naked.

She patted his hand with her other one. "As long as you promise." She took one more bite of the oatmeal, ruffled his hair, and dumped the dish in the sink. "Do the dishes for me?"

He nodded.

Before she left, she plopped the *Craft* in front of him and tapped it. "They need someone to do Tarot readings for Beltane at the Crooked Knot."

"Thanks."

When he'd finished eating and scraped out the remains of her oatmeal into the garbage disposal, he called the Crooked Knot and at first, didn't make any headway getting to the owner until he said, "This is, uh, it's West Archer. Diana's son?"

"Diana...? Oh!" said the person on the other end, some poor barista who probably had a dozen irate customers that needed their vegan lattes and kombucha more than he needed to talk to the owner.

"Yara's the owner, right? Can I talk to her?"

"Sure, sure, one second."

He heard the barista set down the phone and about a minute later, the owner answered, "Westley?"

"Hi, Yara."

"How are you?"

"Good, fine."

"What's going on?"

"I saw you needed someone to do Tarot readings? For Beltane?" He rubbed his eyes, hating that he'd resorted to name-dropping like this.

"Really? Diana says you hate doing Tarot readings."

That was true. It wasn't anything about the cards themselves or his ability to do it, but it was impossible to do good readings on people who weren't honest with him and honest people were hard to come by. "Not as much as I hate being broke. Listen, I've got some references if you want them."

"For doing Tarot?" Yara asked, a laugh in her voice.

"No, just. You know, in general."

"It pays a hundred bucks. All night. Eight to one."

"Eight to...Eight in the morning?" he asked.

She laughed again. "No, West, honey, eight at night. A hundred bucks and all the coffee you can drink."

"Alright. Thanks, Yara."

"No problem, honey. Say hi if you see your mom."

"I will."

"Bye now."

He hung up after a mumbled goodbye. Yara would probably see his mother before he did. They'd been sleeping together on and off for a few months. His mother had about a dozen different casual partners scattered throughout the state and he'd given up keeping track of which one, or ones, she was seeing currently.

The only he really had to remember was Burton because things had ended badly with him and therefore, he was never to be spoken of.

He went over to the calendar and flipped to April and jotted down *crooked knot 8 pm* under the thirtieth.

A hundred dollars. In about a month. That wasn't nearly enough.

Not that Laurel hounded him about rent. She didn't even ask when she knew he hadn't found much work that month.

He returned to perusing the *Craft* and placed about a dozen more phone calls. A lot of old ladies wanted help getting their gardens ready for spring now that they'd had a few warm weeks in a row. He wrote down all their names and addresses, how much they'd wanted to pay him and when he was supposed to be there.

One of them was Hezzie Jacobs, who lived a literal stone's throw away from them. When he called her about her garden, she talked to him for a full forty-five minutes, letting him know how all the grandchildren she never saw were doing. He told her he would come by this afternoon and vaguely dreaded the number of snickerdoodles she would try to feed him.

At least the gardening would burn off those calories.

Maybe more than burn them off. Hezzie had a vast garden and turned a tidy profit every summer selling her crops to those who had a less-than-green thumb. There was something about the quality of her herbs that boosted the power of spells and lent a richer quality to whatever food to which they'd been added. Of course, sometimes that could go awry, he recalled, thinking of the time Laurel had made spaghetti sauce from tomatoes and basil from Hezzie's garden. She'd accidentally produced an absolutely delicious love potion that should not have been consumed in large servings and definitely not at a potluck.

Especially not at a pot luck where children had been present.

West, who had luckily been cutting carbs that summer, had ended up rounding up all the children and herding them to the nearest park to avoid any kind of childhood trauma that might have come from witnessing what had basically turned into a backyard orgy.

HIS LUNCH of steamed chicken and broccoli was made tolerable by doubling the amount of garlic the recipe had required.

The doorbell rang and he continued flossing, assuming it was some UPS package for Laurel. She may have denied her addiction to online shopping, but she had something delivered at least once a week and he was never convinced that she needed any of the things she'd bought.

The doorbell rang again so he gave his teeth a final inspection and went to the door. He peeked out through the curtain, checking for Mormons.

Instead, he saw the man from before.

He had totally forgotten. He heaved a sigh and pulled open the door. He only opened it partway and blocked his entrance to the house with his body.

"What?" West demanded.

"You said to come back later."

"Fine."

The man stared for a second, then cleared his throat. "I, uh. So...I mean. How's this all work, anyway?"

"You ask questions. I answer."

There was never more to it than that. Thankfully, most of the people who came to see him only came once. Maybe the black coins were hard to come by or maybe there were other people better suited to other kinds of questions.

West held out his hand and the man raised an eyebrow.

"The coin?"

"Oh! Sorry." He fished the coin out of his jacket and placed it in West's palm.

West pocketed it. "What's your question?"

Once again, the man looked around the neighborhood like he was expecting to see binocular-wielding spies hanging from the trees. "It's about a death," he confided softly, not like he had reverence for the dead but like he thought the house might be bugged.

West hated the idea of letting him in, but it had to be better than standing half in the door with the man's gaze darting around.

He opened the door wider and stepped back.

"Thanks."

West nodded towards the kitchen table and the man headed over, his gait somewhere between swagger and shuffle. He left behind a trail of scents, cigarettes and cologne and something else West couldn't identify. He did know that he'd be lighting a candle and opening the windows to get rid of the smell as soon as the man left.

The man glanced back and caught West wrinkling his nose at him.

West turned his eyes away immediately and came over to the table, his arms crossed in his best impatient pose.

"I'm Kit, by the way."

"Great. What's your question?"

"Maybe you saw it on the news? His name's Mike McAuliffe, he passed about a month ago..."

West waited.

"He kind of lived around here, over in West Hartford. He was killed."

Being a brusque dick felt wrong when discussing a murder victim, so West softened his pose a little, uncrossing his arms and arranging his face to be less sour. "You knew him or something?"

"Yeah. Pretty well. Anyway. The cops don't know who did it."

West sighed and explained, "Listen, it doesn't work like that. I don't just *know* things. I can only—"

"You can tell when people are lying."

He nodded. "Something like that."

"Right. Uh. So then, if I tell you something, you'll know if it's true or not?"

"Usually." Some people were exceptional liars and some people convinced themselves of the lie, which clouded West's ability to discern the truth of their statements, but other than that, he could make a liar easier than he could make another queer person.

"People are starting to talk like I was the one who did him in," Kit admitted. "And, you know, the circumstances, they're kind of against me. But I didn't do it, alright? We might...well, things might have been ugly but, shit, not like that."

West nodded.

Kit cleared his throat. "The cops have kind of been asking around about me."

West couldn't blame them. Kit wouldn't have towered above most men and he wasn't brawny, but his presence had a solid feel to it. His aura took up space and, more than that, he drew the eye. Dressed in all back, wickedly disheveled, he just plain *looked* like he was up to no good. Judging by the goat skull inked into his forearm, he probably *was* up to no good.

Kit caught West's gaze lingering on the tattoo and he tugged the sleeve of his jacket down. "So anyway. I didn't do it. I'd like to know who did. Clear this all up."

He likely had other illegal things that he wanted to conceal, but West could tell that Kit was innocent of the murder of Michael McAuliffe, at least. "Alright, fine. But you still haven't asked any questions."

Kit fished around in his jacket and produced a newspaper clipping. He smoothed it out on the table and tapped the third paragraph.

Ms. Luella Copeland, 62, lives in the apartment next to the deceased. On the night of the murder, she saw and heard nothing, despite being home at the time. "It was late," Ms. Copeland shared, "I was in bed. I just hope they find whoever did this to Mike. The poor man's been having such a rough time. He didn't deserve this."

Even if it had been printed in bold red letters, the lies couldn't have been more obvious.

"First of all, Luella knows everything about everyone in the whole apartment building. Second, she hated Mike. It just doesn't sit right."

"She's lying," West confirmed.

"All of it?"

West reached over to take the clipping. He rubbed his finger over the newsprint, smudging the ink somewhat. "It *was* late. She wasn't in bed. And she doesn't hope they find who killed him."

Kit smacked the table. "I knew it. What'd she see?"

West shook his head, feeling bad again. "I told you, it doesn't work like that. I just know what's a lie."

The other man raked a hand through his dark hair and instead of mussing it, somehow managed to make it look better. He leaned back in his chair and West caught a glimpse of a tattoo just below the collar of his shirt.

Not that he was looking.

"Do you have any other questions?"

"Uh." Kit skimmed the article. "This part. When they say they don't have any suspects right now?"

West read the article in full this time. It detailed the circumstances of Mike's death (grisly, violent, beaten with an unusual level of ferocity) and his character (polite, responsible, well-liked). He had lived in the apartment for years and had worked in the same office for years. He had no known enemies. The detective who'd spoken to the paper reported no suspects. West confirmed, "That's a lie, too. Or...sort of."

"Sort of?" Kit asked.

"You know, sort of. A half-truth. Like, the department might not have any official suspects, but they've got ideas. Or...they might have a name, but not think anything of it. Or it might just be that one cop. He might know who he thinks did it."

"Oh." The man gnawed his lip, then reached into his jacket. He pulled his hand back, but West thought he heard the shuffle of a cigarette pack.

They sat at the table, the article between them, and West counted thirty-four seconds according to the loud ticks of the clock over the sink. The other man's eyes were fixed on the clipping, his mouth drawn into a frown.

"Is that it?"

Kit took up the article and stowed it in his jacket. "I guess so."

Usually, people left with more answers. West almost felt bad for him. He began to stand, then settled back into his seat. "You...you're not human."

That took the man by surprise. He fixed his eyes on West's face. "No. Figure I'm not. Thanks for the reminder," came his reply, flat and cool.

West hadn't meant it as a dig, though he saw how Kit could take it as one. Demons, of any variety, weren't exactly welcomed by other members of the Community. The Fallen had a little more luck fitting in than Hell-born creatures or the Devil spawn, but overall the relations weren't ideal. Demons tended to skulk around with vampires, as well as the occasional shapeshifter or lycanthrope; rarely they made friends with witches and mages. They avoided fairies altogether.

"Was this guy? Mike? Was he...?"

"Human?" Kit asked, his brows knitted together.

West nodded.

"As they come. He wouldn't have known the difference between an imp and a werewolf." Kit gave a bit of a smile. "Not even if he got bit."

West asked, "Oh. No Community involvement at all?"

"No."

That was a lie. " 'Cause if he was, that might be why the cops aren't picking anything up. You've got to know creatures scoot under the radar for a lot of things."

"You think a creature did him in?"

West shrugged. He didn't want to put too many ideas into the other man's head, just point out a few things worth considering. "I don't know. It could be a possibility. That's all."

"Alright." Kit nodded. "I guess, well, thanks, I guess. I don't think I've got any more questions."

West nodded.

"That coin. I don't get it back, do I?"

"No." Nobody had ever asked for their coin back.

"Figured. Only good for one visit, huh?"

"Yes," West replied emphatically and ignored the guilty twinge in his gut.

"I guess...I guess I should go talk to Luella."

West shrugged. He didn't give advice to the people who came to ask him questions, or at least, he tried to not to. It wasn't any of his business and he didn't have any intention of striking up friendly relationships with the kind of people who came bearing those wooden coins.

Having one in the first place meant that they'd been trafficking with the Devil and as much as witches had a reputation for it, these days most of them avoided any association with devilry or black magic like the plague.

Outside of the actual Devil-worshipers and evil witches, that was.

Kit stood and headed towards the door. West followed if only to lock it after the demon had left.

He didn't expect the demon to turn and offer him his hand. West shook it begrudgingly, expecting a knuckle-crushing squeeze. "Thanks," Kit told him, his grip firm but not harsh, with no lingering and the right amount of eye contact.

West nodded, suddenly reminded of what his mother had said about judging men by their handshakes.

And then Kit was gone, heading down the front walkway towards the sidewalk. West watched him fish around in his jacket, produce both keys and a cigarette, which he lit without the aid of a lighter or match.

It surprised him to see Kit walk across the street not to the beaten-up green Cavalier or to the sleek and shiny red Audi, but to a mid-sized black Subaru that looked incredibly safe. It looked like it would drive well in the snow and have plenty of room in the backseat for groceries or maybe a dog.

Kit probably had a dog. He looked like the kind of man that would have a dog, a scruffy, ugly mutt of a thing with a butch name and a lolling tongue.

West checked the time and saw that he was late. He grabbed his keys, hurried to lock the door, and ran down the street to Hezzie's house. She opened the door for him as soon as he set foot in her yard.

"Westley! I knew you'd be by, come on in, I made some cookies."

"Oh, Hezzie, that's alright."

"They're fresh," she tempted.

He caved and went inside. He took two cookies, chocolate chip, without hesitation before he remembered that he was on a diet, and turned down the third when she offered it.

"No, Hezzie, that's alright, you're paying me to do the garden, not to eat cookies."

She smiled at him and followed him outside when he went. She pointed out the damage to the raised beds that needed to be repaired, the plant skeletons from last summer that needed to get pulled out, and the autumn leaves that had gotten trapped under an early snowstorm and needed to be cleared out of the drainage areas.

As she pointed them out, he attended to the problems and listened with one ear as she told him about all the things she would have told her children if they'd ever called her.

"And you know, Westley, I always said that if someone's going to leave a job they should always have another one lined up. Everyone has bills to pay, haven't they? But does anyone listen?"

She paused.

"I guess not," he supplied, carefully ripping up a shriveled, thorny stem.

"No, I guess not! He hasn't got any kind of new job lined up and maybe he hated that store, but plenty of people work at jobs they hate. I don't know why he should be so special that he has to love his job."

"I don't know what to tell you, Hezzie," he said and that seemed to satisfy her because she continued on with the saga of Daniel and how he left his job without getting a new one first.

West had left his last job without getting a new one first, but he hadn't exactly quit or been fired. He'd been put on leave until he'd used up all his sick time and then it had been politely suggested that he might want to look for somewhere else to work.

He couldn't have imagined going back to work after everything that had happened and figured it was for the best.

He got by now.

But then again, maybe 'getting by' for two years wasn't getting by at all.

He reached down to yank out another stem and misjudged the placement of his hand. When he pulled the stem, thorns ripped through his palm, scraping off several layers of skin and sending beads of blood welling to the surface.

He hissed, swore under his breath, and shook out his hand.

"Personally, I think he should—Are you alright, Westley?"

He nodded.

"Was that one of the pumpkins? Oh, they're tricky, you know. Come over here, let me take a look at it." She beckoned him over.

He went, feeling more than a little sorry for himself as the scrape started to smart.

"Oh, well, let's get that washed up."

Hezzie took him firmly by the elbow and brought him inside to the sink, where she made him wash his hands using rosemary and hyssop soap, then personally patted the scrapes dry for him. She dabbed on a bit of salve and then said, "I think that's about enough for today, Westley."

"Oh, I can finish it."

"No, no, you know, it's about time for my nap anyway. I'll give you a call later in the week, you can come by and finish it. What did we say it was?" She looked over at the clock. "Ten an hour?"

"Yes."

She handed him another cookie and insisted he eat it. He nibbled at it while she wrote him out a check for twenty-five dollars.

He pocketed it, vaguely floored that anyone wrote checks anymore. "Thanks, Hezzie. And for the cookies. I'll come back and finish everything."

She patted him on the arm and sent him on his way.

Once he got home, he used a magnet to stick the check to the fridge, knowing it would end up in the wash or otherwise lost if he didn't.

He checked his phone, which he had left behind in his hurry, and saw that his sister had texted him screenshots of someone's Facebook photos with a lot of question marks after each one.

He ignored it, sniffed himself, and took a quick shower.

Maybe next time he would see if he could do the yard work in the morning, right after his jog, so he wouldn't have to shower twice.

Not that his time was so valuable that he had better things to do than take a shower. It would have been better for the planet, though.

When Laurel came home, he was seated on the living room floor with his Tarot cards spread in front of him and Mipsy, the rabbit, arranged in front of them.

"You know, it's not a joke," she warned, the frown so audible in her voice that he didn't even have to look up.

"What?" he asked. He tapped the two of swords. "Mipsy, you're going to need to be patient. What you want and what's possible will come together, but it's best to remain silent and evaluate first. Try to remain unprejudiced. That makes sense, given that you've got the two of coins here, in your present. A lot of ups and downs..."

"West."

"You sound just like Mom, you know."

"Stop fooling around with those."

He sighed and swept up the cards. He had to get back into the swing of these by Beltane and he didn't have the guts to do a reading on himself. "You're just mad because I didn't text you back."

"Well! What did you think?" she asked.

"She's cute."

"You say that about *everyone*."

"I'm pansexual, I think everyone's cute," he told her, putting the cards away and returning Mipsy to her hutch.

"Let me set you up with her."

"Laurel..." he sighed.

His sister came over and shoved her phone into his face. "She is funny and really smart, she's got her Master's in social work, you'd like her, West. One date. Come on."

He shrugged.

"She thinks you're cute."

He groaned. "Come on, don't go showing people my pictures, Laurel, that's so weird!"

"It's not that weird."

"It absolutely is, you're my sister, not my pimp." He walked into the kitchen. "Besides, I don't have any money to go on a date right now."

"She's smart, she likes free shit. Go to a museum or something."

"Museums charge admission," he pointed out.

"You're gonna die alone, really, I swear, West." Laurel trudged upstairs.

West thought her proclamation was a little premature. Twenty-seven wasn't old enough to know if he was going to die alone.

Thirty-two, though, might have felt closer to that threshold. It wasn't old but he'd been told that entering the third decade of one's life could have strange effects on the psyche.

Maybe it wasn't him that Laurel should have been trying to set up dates for.

When she came back downstairs, already in her pajamas, he approached with the remote and informed her, "I didn't watch any episodes of *Forensic Files* without you."

She accepted the remote and patted the couch cushion beside her. "If you weren't binge-watching TV, what did you do all day?"

"Not much. You want me to read your cards for you?" he offered.

"No."

"I've got to practice before Beltane," he said.

"Oh, are you doing the Crooked Knot?"

He nodded. "Had to name drop to get it though."

"Ahh, West, if you dedicated yourself, you could run a proper business. If Randy Thompkins can keep open his shop—"

He cut her off, "Randy lives in Salem, anyone can keep open a shop in Salem as long as they stock pentacles, black candles, and dreamcatchers."

"West, you're a good witch. You could make a living out of it," Laurel insisted.

"Maybe."

She reached over and gave his arm a pat. "I bet Mom—"

"No."

"She'd lend you the money," she mentioned, her voice casual.

"I don't want to borrow anything from Mom."

"Alright, alright, fine, forget I said anything," Laurel soothed. "She has a table at the library craft fair on Friday. In Lowell Falls. I'm working, but you should see if she needs help setting up."

"I should," he admitted.

And he would. He snagged his phone from the arm of the couch and texted his mother.

March 30, 2016
Wednesday

AFTER HE'D finished up cleaning out Hezzie's garden and gone for his jog, West was dirty, sweaty, and ravenous. He'd put on his raggediest sweats that morning and when he approached the house to find Kit once again smoking on his front steps, a weird flush of embarrassment rolled through him.

Kit made unkempt look casual and cool. He stood and approached West, his heavy boots scuffing against the flagstones of the walkway. Smoke trailed up from his hand.

"You've got to stop showing up here," West told him.

"I had some more questions."

West grunted. "You already used your coin."

"I know, but—"

"Have you got another one?" West asked.

"No, but—"

"So you can go."

"I can pay you. Real money," Kit told him, a desperate note seeping into his voice.

West had to consider the offer, at least. He thought about his bank account, slim as it was, and weighed the idea of making a few bucks against the idea of spending more time with a literal demon.

He didn't mind seeing them around town or at Community events, but he didn't think getting involved in one's personal affairs would bode well. This was a murder investigation, after all, and though Kit hadn't committed the crime, someone certainly had.

"Two hundred dollars," Kit offered.

"Uhhh." There was no way West could turn that down, no matter what Kit wanted from him. He glanced towards the house. Laurel absolutely wouldn't stand for having a demon in the house, even one as dilute as Kit. "Come back in a little bit. About an hour. I've got to shower."

Kit grunted and took a drag on his cigarette. West thought he was going to argue but he only growled, "Fine," and stalked off towards his car.

Inside Laurel immediately demanded, "What was *that?*"

"Nothing."

"It wasn't nothing," she said.

"Just some guy. He had a question about...a work thing."

Laurel crossed her arms.

"Don't you have to be at work in, like, ten minutes?" he asked.

"Yes! I wasn't about to leave with some *guy* smoking on my porch. What the hell is that about!" she cried. "He *looked* like Devil spawn. He looked sketchy."

He wrinkled his nose. He didn't want her poking into Kit at all. His family didn't know about the deal he'd struck with the Devil and he wanted to keep it that way. Getting a reputation as that kind of witch was the last thing he wanted. "What century is it, Laurel? Devil spawn? Come on. Go to work."

She sighed disgustedly at him, grabbed her pocketbook, and stalked out. Before she left, she warned, "I don't care what kind of work thing it is, I don't want demons hanging around my house."

He rolled his eyes. He didn't like Kit hanging around but he didn't think the man was going to do anything more than litter and make the neighbors gossip.

He could have been wrong, of course. Kit was probably dangerous.

He looked dangerous, anyway.

West tried not to think about Kit anymore as he climbed into the shower. His thoughts turned instead to his mother and the library craft fair. Hawking her jewelry wasn't his idea of a rollicking time but she'd offered to buy him lunch for helping out.

And, he figured, it would get him off the hook for a while.

He wouldn't have minded seeing his mother so much if she wasn't always reading his aura and giving him recommendations about things he didn't want her advice on. She might have been open about her love life, but West could live without knowing which sex positions would open up his sun chakra.

When he dressed, he picked through the dish of jewelry in his room. He'd collected about a thousand rings and bracelets over the years, but the dish housed his favorites. Today he slipped a silver band onto one middle finger and another onto his thumb. His impulse was always to cover himself in jewelry, but he limited himself to the two rings and a few thin leather bracelets. Anything more than that and he worried he'd start looking like his mother, who absolutely dripped with charms and amulets.

The doorbell sounded and he grabbed a hoodie, struggling into it as he jogged up the basement stairs to reach the first floor. Laurel had a finished basement, with its own bathroom, and, though the space lacked natural light and he needed to run the dehumidifier year-round, it was better than any apartment he could afford.

When he opened the door, Kit smiled at him, an amused grin that came with a raised eyebrow.

"What?" West demanded, not liking that smile at all.

"No, just, uh, I like your sweatshirt."

West scowled and glanced down at the hoodie, which did boast a cosmic galaxy pattern and a disembodied cat head floating on the chest, but he'd had it for years and it was the most comfortable thing he owned. "What did you want?"

"Come talk to Luella with me."

West's eyebrows shot up. He'd thought Kit would have more questions, maybe more newspaper clippings, but he would never have made this leap. "Are you kidding?"

"I can't tell when she's lying."

"Absolutely not."

Kit reached into his pocket and pulled out a folded wad of bills. "Two hundred dollars."

It was a sight from which West couldn't take his eyes. It was the largest sum of money he'd been offered in years, except for that one creepy Facebook message he'd gotten last July. It would be stupid not to accept. "It's, it's not going to be dangerous?"

"Luella? She's a bitch but she's not dangerous."

Not a lie. With a sigh and hating himself a little bit, West took the money and stashed it in one of the kitchen drawers. "I don't have a car."

Kit smirked. "So...is this you asking for a ride?"

"Yes."

"You know, I thought witches were trying to go for that whole earthy, openminded vibe these days," Kit commented.

West ignored him as he found his shoes and bent to tie the laces.

"I mean, I'm not saying you're all...eye of newt but—"

"But I'm not trying to heal you with crystals and offering you ten types of herbal tea?" West guessed.

"I was expecting more hippie-dippy than..." Kit glanced him over. "I don't know, that so-ugly-its-cool hipster thing you're going for."

West didn't know if he should be offended, especially considering that if either of them was trying to give off a vibe with their look it had to be the man who wore black from head to toe. He stepped outside and locked the door. "Where are we going anyway? I mean, I know you said West Hartford but...?"

"It's over on Steele Road."

West nodded, not sure what that meant. He didn't know West Hartford as well as he should, but he hadn't gone out of town much when he'd been in high school and he'd gone to college out of state. He'd stayed in Massachusetts until he'd found himself out on his ass and out of a job.

Kit unlocked his car and West braced himself as he got in, expecting the stench of cigarettes, but the car only smelled like air freshener and something else, something fruity. Applesauce, maybe, but he didn't know why a car would smell like applesauce.

There wasn't a hint of cigarette ash in anywhere in the car.

Kit fiddled with his phone and the radio briefly. The first thing that played was a pitchy dance-pop song.

West had to ask, "Isn't this one of the Jonas brothers?"

"Mmm. Joe," Kit mumbled, his eyes still fixed on his phone as he searched for something else. He tapped something else and the music changed to an oppressively, discordantly haunted kind of instrumental music.

After three minutes of no conversation and the overwhelming sound of the music, West asked, "So. What is this?"

"The Kilimanjaro Darkjazz Ensemble," Kit said, "Self-titled album."

"Oh."

West looked out the window and watched the house pass by. He wondered what Laurel would think if she knew he'd gone with this guy. He decided that he wouldn't mention it.

"You..."

Kit looked over when he'd trailed off. "What?"

"How'd you know this Mike guy, anyway?"

According to a brief google search, Michael McAuliffe (it took him three times to spell it right) had been a well-off real estate agent in his mid-forties. The pictures that accompanied West's search showed that Mike was a big guy, tall and beefy, with an open, smiling face. Probably one of those guys that everyone called a big teddy bear.

West couldn't see how a grungy scoundrel like Kit fit into his life at all. Drug-dealer, he guessed.

Kit's hands shifted on the wheel and he cleared his throat. "Ummm."

Definitely his drug dealer, West decided.

"He..." Kit sighed. "He was my ex."

"Oh!" West nearly shouted. He hadn't meant to be so loud, but the confession had been the last thing he'd expected. He hadn't gotten a whiff of queerness off Kit. "Oh. I'm, uh, I'm sorry for your loss."

"Yeah, well, we split a while ago."

"Sorry." West didn't know what else to say. "People think you killed him?"

"It was ugly."

"Breakups can get like that."

Kit snorted. "Yeah, well, divorces are worse."

That absolutely didn't compute. Not only had Kit been in a relationship with a clean-cut, well-off guy like Mike, not only was he gay, but he was *divorced*. West couldn't imagine Kit ever planning a wedding or proposing. He couldn't even imagine him sticking around for an entire night after hooking up with someone.

That explained Kit's lie from before, though, about Mike not being involved with the Community. Marrying a demon certainly qualified as involvement.

It didn't surprise him that they'd gotten divorced, apparent differences aside. Immortals didn't tend to make good life partners, especially not for humans. The difference in lifespan made things too weird and creatures like demons and vampires almost always came with a lot of baggage and a lot of exes.

"May-December romances, you know, they're hard to manage," West offered as a bit of consolation. He'd gone on a date with a twenty-one-year-old last winter and it had been like hanging out with a space alien and he was only twenty-seven. He couldn't imagine what it would be like to date someone who had been born in an entirely different century.

Kit frowned. "What?"

"I mean. Making it work with someone who's got to be, like, a fourth your age. That's what I've heard, anyway. Some of the people I've read cards for..." West trailed off, realizing how badly he'd been blabbering.

"I'm thirty-nine," Kit informed him.

"Oh. I."

"Yeah."

Neither of them spoke until Kit parked inside the gated lot; he'd needed to get buzzed in and the gateman had seemed wary of letting him in.

West lingered awkwardly behind the other man as he got them through the other doors, into the apartment building, and up to the third floor.

Once there, he knocked aggressively on one of the doors.

They got no answer.

Kit knocked again and called, "Luella, get out here."

The door opened to reveal a woman in her sixties, dressed in an immaculate teal pantsuit. West was almost surprised to see that she didn't wear a matching pillbox hat on top of her stiff hair, which had been dyed an unnatural, flat shade of brown. "You don't live here anymore, I'm going to call the police if you keep bothering me."

"Luella."

"I'm going right now," she threatened and began to close the door.

"I just need to know what you saw," Kit insisted, putting a hand on her door so she couldn't close it more. "Please."

"I already told you I didn't see anything."

"That's a lie," West said.

"Excuse me?" she asked, looking over him.

West was pretty sure he actually saw her lip curl at the sight of him. "That's a lie. You did see something."

"Young man, I don't know who you think you are—"

"What did you see?" Kit demanded.

West glanced at him and caught eyes with him, giving what he opened to be a meaningful look. "Did you see a lot of people that night?"

"No."

Truth. "Did you hear a struggle?"

"No, I didn't hear anything."

Lie. "You saw one person or more than one?"

The woman squirmed under his questions and she tried to close the door again. "I'm going to call the police."

She wasn't going to call the police. She was hiding something, West would have put money on it. "No, you aren't. What are you hiding? What did you see?"

The older woman appeared somewhat shaken now and he felt bad for pursuing this so relentlessly, but if someone had been killed then she shouldn't have been covering things up. No matter that he'd never known Michael McAuliffe, his murder shouldn't have gone unsolved. Who knew if the person was still out there menacing other people?

Luella tried to pull the door closed but Kit held firm.

West pressed, "Did you see more than one person?"

"No!"

That was true. "Did you see a man?"

"No, I didn't—"

True. To Kit, he said, "It was a woman, then. Or, well, you know there aren't just the two genders but..." He glanced at Luella and didn't imagine she knew that there was more to the world than male and female. "Did you know the woman you saw?"

"No."

True. She hadn't known the woman, but she had seen her. "Will you at least tell us what she looked like?"

Asking a series of yes/no questions would eventually get him answers but it was a lengthy process that involved being able to think of all the specifics. For getting descriptions of people, it became an intense game of Guess Who?

Is your person wearing a hat? Do they have glasses? Did they have blond hair? Does your person have a mustache?

It worked well enough unless he forgot to ask if someone was thin or if they had scars or a particular hairstyle.

"Listen, the sooner you tell us about her, the sooner we can go," West reasoned.

"Please," Kit said again and seemed genuinely distressed.

Of course, if the cops thought he'd killed his ex-husband, he had a good reason for wanting answers out of her. Especially if they'd had a bad divorce. Every procedural crime show West had ever watched had an eighty percent chance of ending with the victim's domestic partner behind bars.

"You can tell us or I can keep asking you questions," West told her.

The woman sighed and gave the two of them scathing looks. "I barely saw anything."

"Height, weight...anything," West requested.

"She was...short. Maybe five feet tall. Sturdy. Dark hair, too. She had her hair tied back in one of those tight ponytails. I couldn't make out what they were shouting about, not really."

"You heard something," West told her.

She redoubled her glare. "Something about a deal they'd made. I can't remember all of it."

"Alright." She'd told the truth and West didn't get the sense she was holding anything back. "That's it?"

"Yes."

That was true. He stepped away from the door and nodded for Kit to let her go back into the apartment. She didn't have anything else to tell them and he was absolutely starving. He didn't want to stand around here any longer playing twenty questions, feeling shabby and cheap compared to the classy neutrals and plush hall carpeting.

Kit stepped back and Luella snapped the door closed, telling them, "Next time I'm calling the police," before she slammed the door.

"She's not calling the police," West said.

Kit let out a half-chuckle. "I could have told you that. She's called the cops so many times they've started writing her up for it. They fined her once, too, I think."

West's stomach let out an aggressive gurgle. He hadn't eaten breakfast.

That was fine, he reasoned, it was almost time for lunch and he'd eaten too much for dinner last night anyway.

"There's a good bagel place down the street," Kit informed him.

"I'm fine."

The demon made a face but didn't say anything else. As they walked out, he kept his eyes trained straight ahead and West understood why when he saw the bits of police tape still stuck to the frame of one door.

The murder had been weeks ago and West wondered how long it took for everything to be processed.

He wondered how long it took to clean up a crime scene afterward and who had to pay for it.

Absolutely inappropriate things to be wondering, of course.

His phone buzzed and he checked it.

"Ohh, that's a good face," Kit commented.

"It's my mom."

The demon nodded understandingly.

West texted his mother back, assuring her that he'd be ready on time Friday morning. She always got like this, asking him a thousand times if he'd packed everything, paid his bills, remembered to turn the stove off, things like that.

"We're doing this thing together Friday and she's told me when to be ready at least ten times already," he said.

"Sucks," Kit agreed, not dismissive but sympathetic. "Listen, are you sure you don't want some coffee or something? I could use some caffeine."

"Go ahead."

Kit stopped at the bagel place and West followed him in; he didn't want to, but it would have been weirder to sit alone in his car and wait for him to come back. Initially, he hung back but when a group of businessmen came in, all of them magazine-perfect with their tailored suits and even smiles, West scooted up into line beside Kit.

"Change your mind?" Kit asked.

He shrugged. "I don't know, whatever."

Kit didn't try to talk to them again, not until they'd gotten back in the car and started to drive.

"Listen, uh, thank you."

"Hmm?" West had scalded his tongue on his coffee and had been dwelling on how he always burned his tongue and should probably give up on hot beverages altogether.

"For coming. You didn't have to."

"You paid me," West reminded.

"Still. I appreciate it," he said. "I'm...I'm just trying to get some closure on all this."

"And avoid getting arrested," West pointed out.

"Well, yeah, and that but...I mean. Things went to shit but that doesn't mean I didn't still care about Mike."

That was true. Very true. "You guys were together for a long time?"

"Married for ten years, dated for a few before that."

Longer than West would have guessed. "Uh. This is probably personal..."

"Go ahead, I'm fine with personal."

That was a lie. "No, you aren't," West argued.

"Just go ahead and ask," Kit told him.

"I mean, living forever and marrying a human, how did you think that was going to pan out?" West asked.

Kit looked over at him, his dark red-brown eyes holding West's gaze for longer than could have been safe while driving. "I'm not going to live forever."

"Don't demons...? I thought you guys were immortal."

The man snorted. "Sure, some of them. The ones who are, you know, really related to the Devil, but, I mean...my grandma only lived to be a hundred and fifty. And she *looked it*, you know. She aged. Maybe she didn't look that old, but she wasn't a spring chicken. You're thinking of, you know, people who are halves or quarters. I'm not even a sixteenth. Probably not even a sixty-fourth."

"Oh."

"So, you know, I'll definitely make it to a hundred and I can do a couple of magic tricks, but I'm not going to be seeing what the thirty-first century has to offer."

West took another sip of his coffee and didn't burn his tongue this time. He'd known that demons had weaker powers as their line of decent became more diluted, but he hadn't known that it applied to their life expectancies as well.

"I couldn't imagine living that long anyway," Kit admitted.

"Mmm."

"All the vampires go crazy."

"Most of them, yeah," West agreed. Immortality was a rough lot in life; some creatures handled it better than others, but vampires had a tough time. West thought it had something to do with the difficulty that came with managing a need for the blood of the living.

Kit pulled into the driveway instead of parking across the street. "Anyway. Thank you again."

"Mmm."

"Maybe—"

West opened the car door. "You need to stop coming around here, though."

"Uh...alright." Kit straightened up and raked his hand through his hair. "Sorry to have bothered you."

"Yeah, it's just, I'm not, you know, a cop or anything. You should tell them what you know. Let them handle it," West insisted. He almost felt bad for not helping more, but he was telling the truth. He had no idea how to deal with this.

Kit fixed his eyes on West's face and pronounced, "You're the only one who believes me."

"Drop an anonymous tip or something." West got out of the car, his face flushing and his voice louder than it needed to be as he explained, "Listen. I'm a witch, alright? I do good-luck spells and protection charms. I'm...I help my mom sell her handcrafted jewelry and do Tarot readings on Beltane. I am not cut out for your...whatever it is that you've got going on." He gestured vaguely in Kit's direction. "Alright?"

"Sure. Sorry. I just...You know. Never mind. You're right."

He closed the door and went towards the house, not looking back until he'd gotten inside and locked the door. He peeked through the curtain to see that Kit lingered in the driveway, leaning forward over his steering wheel for a second before he backed out and zipped down the street, not exactly speeding but definitely pushing his luck.

April 1, 2016
Friday

THE CRAFT fair started at ten, but West's mother picked him up at seven a.m. exactly. West could usually make himself get up in the morning without much difficulty but compared to his mother, he was a night owl. She woke up every morning at four a.m. to do yoga and had for as long as he could remember.

When she picked him up, she handed him a mason jar of overnight oats that smelled strongly of honey and peanut butter.

"Eat," she demanded when he took the jar and didn't immediately guzzle it down.

He sighed, found a spoon, and ate on the drive over, wondering how many calories this accidental second breakfast had.

"You're getting so skinny."

"I'm not," he said.

"Westley."

"Christ, Mom, I ate the oatmeal, alright?"

"You need to be taking better care of yourself," she admonished. "Your body is the only thing you're always going to have, huh? You need to treat it right."

"I do. What's so wrong with wanting to lose a few pounds?" he demanded.

"You're always wanting to lose a few pounds."

"No, I just. I have a weight I want to get to, okay? It's not a big deal." He had an exact number in mind and sometimes he could reach that weight and maintain it for a while, but something always interrupted his life and sent him back up ten or fifteen pounds.

She frowned at him. "Laurel says she's been trying to set you up with a girl she knows from work."

"She has been."

"Are you going to let her?"

"Mom, I didn't come to rehash all my conversations with Laurel with you. You're not my therapist," he said, wishing he'd stayed home. "Can we just talk about something else? Literally anything else?"

"Yara mentioned you're doing Tarot readings for Beltane."

"I am."

His mother smiled. "That's good, West, you always did have a gift, you know. You could be a good witch...a *better* witch; you could buckle down and make something of yourself."

"I do plenty of jobs. I get by fine." A week didn't go by without him working some kind of spell; just because he didn't own a storefront or an Etsy page or do bogus Tarot readings over the phone didn't mean he wasn't a good witch. He'd had this conversation with her plenty of times.

Witchcraft didn't always have to be a career. Laurel did perfectly fine as a florist.

The problem, of course, was that he didn't have a career. Not anymore. He'd been telling himself that he would get back into things, but he'd stopped believing it a year and a half ago. He'd told other people that office work just hadn't been right for him, which had been true; he'd hated the cubicles and the harsh lighting and the endless sound of phone calls.

He'd tolerated it, though, because Danny Novak had worked there. Danny Novak, who'd gotten him the job when he'd graduated, who'd been the first and only partner he'd ever lived with, who'd hooked up with him in the closet at the office holiday party for three years in a row.

Danny Novak, who'd dumped him for the office manager and called it trading up.

West twisted the silver band around his forefinger, trying to think of anything else because that had been two years ago. He was over Danny, he told himself, but he wasn't over getting dumped.

At the library, he struggled with the folding table, not able to figure out how to make the legs stay stiff until his mother pointed out the obvious locking mechanism. After that, he spent his time carefully laying out the various pieces she had brought, trying to group them in a way that made sense. Eventually, he had things arranged by material then price and had to stop himself from fiddling with the arrangement anymore.

"West, can you double-check and make sure everything has a price tag?" his mother asked, handing him a pen and a handful of tags.

He nodded and checked all the pieces.

Out of the corner of his eye, he saw an elbow that made his head swivel. He straightened up to see a silhouette that he recognized immediately. It was hard not to, that leather jacket, the combat boots, and all in black.

Kit stood beside a folding table on the other side of the library lawn, one hand shoved into his back pocket and the other one gesturing vaguely as he spoke to a towering Hispanic man holding a box.

West abandoned his task and stalked over to the demon. "Hey."

"You can just put it..." Kit turned around and glanced over him. "Hey."

"What are you doing here?" West demanded, not believing that the other man had had the gall to follow him around like this.

"What?" the demon asked, an eyebrow raised.

"I told you, I'm not helping you anymore."

"Um. Alright." A smug sort of grin spread over Kit's face. "But, you know, I hate to break it to you, I am actually here for another reason."

It was true and immediately West felt like an asshole, his stomach starting to churn. "You, um..."

Kit put his hand into the box the towering man had set down and pulled out a pack of notecards bundled with twine. The notecards had 'thank you' written across the front in delicate calligraphy and around the words was a border of watercolor flowers. Kit flashed the notecards at West, then tossed them on the table. "We've all got bills to pay."

"I..."

Kit gave him an understanding smile that still managed to be patronizing.

"You're an artist?"

"Ugh. I guess."

"You guess?" West asked.

"Artist is so vague."

The tall man started unpacking the box, taking out more notecards, as well as journals with embossed leather covers and other assorted types of stationery. Postcards, decorated envelopes, and paper for letter writing with tasteful headers and borders. Paperweights and coasters that looked like they'd been handmade and hand-painted. They were all, honestly, beautiful.

West rubbed the back of his neck.

"This is my partner, Aarón," Kit offered, jabbing a thumb towards the other man.

"Business partner," Aarón corrected.

"Yeah, sorry, business partner," Kit agreed with an eye-roll. "He lets me hawk my shit at his farm stand and I let him hawk his soap—"

"And candles," Aarón said.

"And candles," Kit amended, "On my online store."

True, all of it, which made West an absolute asshole. He looked at the notecards again.

"And lotion."

"Yes, and lotion, Aarón, and lip balm and sugar scrubs," Kit listed. "Did I miss anything?"

Aarón didn't answer, but he did scowl mightily in Kit's direction before he returned to unpacking the box.

West grimaced.

"Ah, he's alright," Kit assured. "Just grumpy."

"Mhm."

"Anyway. I've got to set up," Kit mentioned which West took as a polite way to say goodbye.

"Sorry."

Kit smiled broadly at him and West took a few steps back, his thoughts tumbling over each other as he realized he had one more question to ask.

"So wait."

Kit paused with his hand halfway into the box.

"So you live in town?" West asked. Only local businesses were allowed to set up tables at the craft fair.

"Uh, yeah," Kit said like it should have been obvious. "Lowell Falls has got the best Community scene in the state. Well, I mean, unless you can afford to live by the shore, which I can't. And New

Avondale is basically one big cow farm."

West had an aunt who lived in New Avondale and could appreciate the sentiment; some kids had gone to summer camp, but he'd been sent there for most of his childhood and teenage summers.

"You, however," Kit began, "Don't live in town."

"No. Well. Devonport is part of Lowell Falls," West pointed out. "It's, uh, a village?"

"I feel like I should have known that."

West nodded and turned around, keeping his eyes on the ground and not looking back. He returned to check the price tags on his mother's jewelry, trying to pretend that he hadn't accused a man of stalking him.

He should have expected that Kit lived locally. Community members tended to flock together, even the ones that didn't get along. It was better for a vampire to live alongside a witch and it was better for a fairy to share their stretch of wood or river with a werewolf or a shifter than it would be for either of them to live alongside ordinary humans. The exception seemed to be in big cities; creatures and magic workers absolutely flocked to places like New York, rubbing elbows with normal people with hardly anyone the wiser.

Not that regular humans didn't live in town, of course, plenty of them did, but the more members of the Community there were in one place, the better they could watch out for each other. It always started with werewolves. Wherever there was one werewolf, others were bound to follow, and by the time half a dozen werewolves had moved into a neighborhood, a mage or a vampire or something else unnatural would be along in a year or two.

"Who was that you're talking to?" his mother asked.

"Just some guy." He glanced over at Kit, then turned his eyes away.

She stared across the lawn for a while, her eyes locked onto Kit as he unpacked everything, carefully arranging his wares, stepping back every so often then going back in to move a stack of notecards or a candle over half an inch.

"He looks...West, he looks like a demon," she pronounced carefully.

"Probably because he is."

"Westley."

"Mother."

"You aren't trafficking with demons, are you?" she demanded.

"Trafficking with...Mom, come on, what *century* is it? The only things that get trafficked anymore are drugs...and sex slaves." He didn't want to talk about this and he didn't want his mother to have even an inkling that he'd made a deal with the Devil.

She would have absolutely lost her mind.

Laurel might have even kicked him out if she knew that his occasional weird visitors came bearing coins granted to them by He Himself. It would be as bad as trying to come out in one of those countries where they still beheaded gay people.

Well, no, it wouldn't be that bad.

"They're not a joke, Westley," his mother warned severely, her voice holding none of her usual good nature or warmth.

"He's barely even a demon," he insisted. "There's got to be at least seven generations between him and the Devil."

His mother crossed her arms and opened her mouth, probably to warn him that demons were dangerous.

"Besides, he's just some random guy, I didn't expect to see him here so I went to, to you know, to say hi," he told her.

"Mmhm."

West glanced at his phone and saw that it would be ten soon and sent up a silent prayer for someone to come over to their table. Someone who would ask about the properties of citrine and rose quartz, who would want to know what each symbol and charm meant. Someone to get his mother talking about something other than demons.

Customers came eventually and as the sun crept higher in the sky, the day grew warmer. Working in an office never afforded him moments like this, beautiful, warm spring days that he got to spend outside. He'd always liked being outside.

"I need something for my sister, her birthday's coming up," a young woman told him, pulling him out of his contemplation of the bird calls coming from the various trees that dotted the library lawn.

"What does your sister like?"

"Blondes," she told him, her fingers trailing over an amethyst bracelet.

"Fresh out of blondes, sorry," he said. "What else does she like?"

"She plays varsity lacrosse for her high school."

His hand immediately went to a carnelian pendant. He handed it over to her and she took it, studying it for a while.

"What kind of stone is this?" she asked.

"That's carnelian, dear," his mother said, floating over to them, as though it was a question West couldn't answer.

He sighed but stepped back. His mother was a better salesperson and it was her jewelry anyway. She had every right to talk to people about it.

Around two, the craft fair started to wind down. His mother had started to pack up the remainder of the pieces she'd brought, and West attempted to organize the cash drawer and the pile of handwritten receipts.

He looked up when he heard the firm sound of booted footsteps and smelled cigarettes. Kit approached, cigarette dangling between his fingers but not lit yet.

"You can't smoke here," his mother said immediately, her voice filled up with disgust she usually reserved for able-bodied people who took handicapped parking spots.

The demon glanced her way and placed the cigarette between his lips. He didn't light it though, just took an envelope out of the back pocket of his jeans and handed it over to West.

The day had warmed considerably, making it too warm for a leather jacket. Kit's arms were bare and showed even more tattoos. The goat skull West had noticed last time, as well as a large moth and a crow. What looked like a bunch of wildflowers covered one forearm, detailed botanical drawings that left hardly any trace of his original skin color. Seeing all of Kit's tattoos probably would have been a lengthy process; West doubted they stopped at his arms.

Kit asked, "How'd you make out?"

West peeled his eyes away from Kit's arms and took the envelope the demon offered, not sure what it could be. Penned in neat, all-capital letters Kit had written WEST. "Fine. Good, actually. You?"

West fiddled with the envelope then slipped it inside the hoodie he'd discarded earlier. He hoped that putting it out of sight would make his mother forget to ask about it.

"Ah, you know, I've had better sales. Left most of my best stuff at home, I didn't think it would go over well at a family-oriented event," Kit shared. "In fact, the library director made it *explicitly* clear that it wouldn't."

His mother glared at Kit then took a box of jewelry from the table and stalked to the car, muttering under her breath the whole time.

"So...did I do something to the two of you specifically or...?" Kit asked. "Is it just a witch thing?"

"She's just, you know, she's worried I'm gonna end up involved in black magic or something if I start talking to demons."

"Does that make me the witchcraft equivalent of a gateway drug?" Kit asked.

A surprised bit of laughter escaped West's lips. He had no idea what to say to that, but it turned out he didn't need to say anything at all.

"I usually hang out at local elementary schools and menace small children, so if you're ever looking to score some nightshade or hex bags, hit me up."

"Yeah, uh, I'll definitely do that," West said with a roll of his eyes.

Kit walked away after that, lighting his cigarette as he went, using a flame he'd conjured from thin air.

After lunch with his mother, where she spent half the time badgering West about where he'd met Kit and the other half saying that he should buckle down and dedicate himself to the craft, West was ready for a nap.

More than ready. He felt entitled. He hugged his hoodie close to his chest as he made the trek down into the basement and, once he knew he was alone, he fished out the envelope he'd wrapped up in the sweatshirt earlier.

He carefully ripped it open and found a card within. The front bore another watercolor, though this one was a landscape.

West recognized the location, a small waterfall off a local hiking trail. It looked different in the painting though, it had a more verdant, almost dreamy, quality to it, which was not what West recalled. Maybe Kit had gone on a good day, or maybe he'd taken some artistic license with the scene.

He cautiously opened the card, worried about what he would find inside.

In block print, the note read:

THE MORE I THINK ABOUT IT, THE MORE YOU'RE RIGHT THAT IT'S SUPERWEIRD OF ME TO COME TO YOUR HOUSE AND HANG AROUND ON YOUR FRONT STEPS SO I CAN ASK YOU QUESTIONS ABOUT AN ONGOING MURDER INVESTIGATION. I DIDN'T MEAN TO GIVE THE WRONG IMPRESSION, I GUESS I'VE JUST BEEN CAUGHT UP WITH THIS THING ABOUT MIKE. ANYWAY, THANKS FOR YOUR HELP AND SORRY IF I 'CAUSED YOU ANY TROUBLE.

KIT

And beneath his name was a phone number, written in the same handwriting but in blue ink instead of black, like Kit had gone back in and added it on impulse.

On the back of the card, there was a website for what had to be the online store Kit had mentioned. A quick google search brought him to the site and revealed that all of Kit's art was impressive, but some of it was definitely not family-friendly. Some just had an atmospheric gloominess to it, illustrations of animal skeletons and dying plants. Other pieces were outright obscene, covering everything from horror to the erotic, and some that had an uncomfortable mixture of the two.

No, West decided, he definitely wouldn't be calling Kit knowing that he'd drawn something that looked like two dead people eating each other alive during a session of mutual oral sex. He closed the webpage and cleared his search history, in case Laurel got ahold of his phone and figured out the passcode, which she did from time to time.

He didn't need her finding that and he also didn't need to get any further involved with some who did illustrations like that.

He couldn't make himself throw away the card though. The painting really was good, and a quick inspection told him that this wasn't a print, but had been hand-painted. The other man had taken time out of his life to make this, put energy and care into its making, and it would have felt like sacrilege to do anything but prop it up on one of his bookshelves.

Hopefully, Laurel wouldn't notice. She didn't come into the basement often.

April 15, 2016.
Friday

LAUREL HAD gotten her way, which she almost usually did. West was on a date.

Or, he would be on a date soon, if the other half of the arrangement ever showed up. Right now, he was just lurking outside a restaurant he'd never been to, waiting for a woman he'd never met to have dinner with him. He checked his phone every thirty seconds or so, checking the time and to see if she'd texted him.

He thought that hanging out on Facebook wasn't a good first impression, but he gave up on first impressions after ten minutes of waiting.

"Westley?" came a clear, pleasant voice from his left.

He looked over to see the woman from the photos with which Laurel had been bombarding him. She looked different, but not in a bad way, but in the way that everyone looked different from the pictures they decided to share on the internet.

Right away, he noticed she had crooked teeth, which explained the tight-lipped, guarded smile in all of the photos he'd seen.

"Yeah, hi," he said. "Leah, right?"

"It's Leia."

"Oh, sorry. My bad."

"No, it's fine," she assured, "People mix it up all the time."

He nodded towards the restaurant. "You, um, you want to have a seat? I got reservations."

"Yeah, sure," she agreed.

Once they'd settled into their seats, West stared down at the menu, which had far too many pages in his opinion.

"So, you, you're Laurel's brother, right?" Leia asked.

"Yeah." He didn't look up from the menu. People always asked that; he had started to use the follow-up questions as a litmus test for whether or not he wanted to spend any more time with that person. *Are you adopted? Different dads, huh? Like, really related, or…?*

Leia he had to give the benefit of the doubt, though, because his sister insisted that she would be perfect for him.

"So, um. You come here a lot?" he asked when he'd finally read through the entire menu and she hadn't asked anything else about his relation to Laurel.

"Yeah, I love this place, their pizza is to die for."

West hadn't seen pizza on the menu and had to go back and double-check. He found it listed on the back. "Did you wanna split a pizza?"

"You can get whatever you want," she assured quickly. She tucked a bit of auburn hair behind her ear and gave him a small smile.

He stared at the menu some more. That smile should have done more to him; West never liked to narrow things down enough to say he had a type, but Leia definitely fell within the category of 'yes, please' when it came to partners. "You work next to Laurel, right?"

"Yeah, at the bakery. But that's, well, you know, it's part-time. I just finished up my Master's, I'm looking for work in the field."

"Oh."

She nodded, took a sip of water, then told him, "I had this idea that I was going to work fulltime *and* do grad school, but I burned out after, like, one semester. I'm looking forward to getting back into the swing of things though. I miss working with kids."

He nodded and tried to think of something to say in response to that.

"What about you?" she asked, "What did you go to school for?"

"History," he said and didn't elaborate. He didn't like to think about how he'd wasted his time in school. History classes had been interesting and going to college out of state had been his first opportunity to get away from the shadow of the Archer family name, to be someone other than Diana's Son or Laurel's Brother.

Leia nodded.

They bantered back and forth like that for a while, both of them trying to find purchase on the conversation and both of them failing. Leia didn't go to the movies much and West hardly watched Netflix. She liked to read but he hadn't heard of any of the books she'd mentioned. She followed the news and he barely knew who was running for president.

They ordered a pizza and she was right, it was good.

It gave her the chance to talk about the semester abroad she'd done in Italy. That was a conversation he could add to, he'd written his share of papers on the ancient Mediterranean world.

"You know," she announced suddenly.

"Hmm?"

"I don't think you ever told me what you do for work."

"Oh." West shrugged. "You know. Odd jobs. Witch stuff."

"Witch stuff?" she asked, her eyebrows up so high they'd disappeared into her bangs. "What's witch stuff?"

"You know. Spells and, um, charms." He didn't know how to explain the craft to people who didn't already have some frame of reference for it. To people outside the Community, witchcraft was folklore or some made-up religion for crunchy granolas. Mages, with their arcane magic, could do plenty of showy party tricks to demonstrate their power but the best West could do was cure someone's cold as proof of his authenticity.

She laughed. "I knew Laurel was into all that New Age stuff but I didn't know you were too. Witch stuff. That's funny."

Curing the common cold should have gotten witches more credit. There wasn't anyone else who could do it reliably. "Yeah, uh. I guess."

Leia rushed to tell him, "No, no, I'm sorry, I didn't mean it like that. I didn't. I just. You know. You don't *look* like you'd be into that stuff."

He took a bite of the pizza crust, thinking about calories and wanting to go home. He chewed thoroughly and washed it down with a bit of water.

Leia was pretty, Laurel had been right about that much. Even her crooked teeth had their own charm. He should have been enjoying himself on this date and the fact that he wasn't seemed to drive the point home: it was him that was the problem. It wasn't that he just hadn't met anyone, it was the fact that he was unwilling to do anything more than show up and hope for the best.

"What's a witch supposed to look like?" he asked.

Leia fumbled for a response. "You know. All. Hippie-dippy. Or super goth, I guess."

He nodded. Not like him. Not male and not half-Asian (or possibly half-Hispanic, though he was really leaning towards Asian these days, and his mother agreed. She thought she remembered there being an 'Eastern fellow' at the party where West had been conceived).

"One of my friends in high school got all into Tarot cards and Ouija boards," she offered.

"Yeah, a lot of kids go through that phase." He fiddled with the last piece of crust but didn't take a bite. He wasn't hungry anymore. "You have any pets?"

"A dog."

Perfect. Pets were always good for at least ten minutes of conversation. "What kind of dog?" he asked.

His question was rewarded with a full fifteen minutes of conversation; he learned all about her dog, Suzy, a lab-shepherd mix who'd been abandoned and tied to a guardrail as a puppy. In return, he told her about Mipsy, who was Laurel's rabbit, but it was better than not saying anything at all.

Eventually, they ran out of things to say, paid the bill, and agreed to call each other. Leia said she'd had a great time, which was nice of her, but only partly true.

West arrived home by ten and had climbed in his pajamas by ten-fifteen. He snuggled into bed and spent a while on his phone, adding Leia as a friend on Facebook, because it seemed the polite thing to do.

His eyes went to the thank-you card Kit had given him and, not for the first time, he thought about checking to see if Kit had a social media presence. He didn't, telling himself that he didn't want anything more to do with the demon.

Kit had had the decency to stay away and a little bit of internet snooping revealed that the police still hadn't made any arrests. They still claimed to have no suspects, but that felt like more of a lie than it had last time West had read the words.

Maybe the demon had done the sensible thing and told the police the information they'd gleaned from Luella.

He hoped so.

His eyes went back to the card.

No one who'd come to ask him questions had ever written him a thank-you card before and he'd definitely been rude to Kit.

He turned off his phone and rolled onto his side, facing away from the card so he would be able to put it out of mind.

By the morning, Leia had accepted his friend request and when he went upstairs for breakfast, Laurel grilled him about every detail of his date.

"You ever think you should just go on your own date instead of living vicariously through mine?" he asked.

She threw him a dirty look.

"What? Don't look at me like that, it's not my fault you're obsessed with a married man," he told her. It came out nastier than he'd meant it, but she'd been thirsting over her best friend since high school. She'd never asked him out and he'd gone on with his life blithely unaware of Laurel's affections.

At this point, West didn't even feel bad for her anymore. She'd had lots of chances to ask out Richard and she'd avoided all of them, always worried about ruining their friendship or making things awkward.

"I'm not obsessed. I don't even feel that way about Richard anymore."

A lie. He didn't need any special intuition to know that, it was scrawled all over her face. "Alright, sure, and the Pope isn't Catholic."

"Shut up, West, what do you know, anyway?"

He kept his mouth shut.

"I know everything is one big joke to you but—"

He cut her off, "Everything is *not* a joke to me." To soften the harshness of his tone, he added, "I'm sorry I said anything about Richard. I know it's touchy."

Best to nip this in the bud before she could go on one of her diatribes about how he was wasting all his potential, about how she and Mom just wanted him to do better for himself.

"I'm not the one still licking my wounds over getting dumped," she snarled.

West opened his mouth, then closed it. He deserved that. He speared a piece of melon, chewed it, then asked, "Plans for Beltane?"

"Mom and I are going to the Bowdens', they're having a bonfire."

He nodded. The Bowdens' had a bonfire every year, they owned a huge tract of land and ended up hosting a lot of parties. Parties that usually turned into ragers and occasionally crossed the line into skyclad sex parties. But only occasionally.

The Crooked Knot would host a tamer affair.

There had been a time when West had gotten excited for holidays; he couldn't pinpoint exactly when he'd started to get diminishing returns on holiday spirit, but it had happened long before he'd gone away to college.

For a while, he'd thought it was just part of growing up, but his mother had never been less than ecstatic to celebrate anything.

"It'll be going on all night, you can probably come by after you do the readings," Laurel offered.

"Maybe."

"Come on, Beltane's only once a year. The weather's supposed to be gorgeous," she wheedled.

"Yeah, maybe," he repeated, "I'll see how I'm feeling."

She got up to put her plate in the sink and gave his shoulder a squeeze, then swooped in to kiss the top of his head. "I'm glad your date with Leia went well."

He gave her a smile and didn't know how to tell her that they'd both been lying when they'd promised to call each other soon.

April 30
Saturday

YARA HUGGED him as soon as he walked in the door, a big warm hug that enveloped him and got him better acquainted with her breasts than he had ever expected to be. Yara stood a full head and shoulders taller than he did and he had to step back and crane his neck to see her face while she explained everything to him.

She got him a coffee (black, at his request) and showed him the table where he would be parked all night. Off to the right of the stage, close to the band so he would be hard to miss, but not so close that the music would overwhelm the readings.

"Oh, and here." Yara handed him a paper coffee cup, one that had *TIPS* scrawled across the front. "Tip jar."

He set it on the table next to his deck of cards.

There were already a dozen people here and he saw a few of them looking in his direction.

"Any questions?" she asked.

"Just one."

"Alright, shoot."

He rubbed the back of his neck. "Um. So. Sometimes readings aren't always...super positive. You want me to bend the truth a little with those ones? I don't want to, you know, ruin the mood or anything, you know?"

"That's fine, West. You know what you're doing," Yara assured.

He'd done this once at a similar type of event and a few people had reacted horribly to their readings. One woman had even burst into tears. He always tried to temper whatever news he had to deliver with a calm voice and reassuring delivery but sometimes, there wasn't a good way to reassure someone when they asked about their pregnancy and the Devil, the Hanged Man, and Death all showed up in one spread.

It wasn't as bad as it looked, of course, the cards had a lot of different meanings but being told, "Death symbolizes a transition, not *literal* death," hadn't done anything to calm the woman or make him feel any better about traumatizing a woman who was seven months pregnant.

West settled in at the table and double-checked his bank account. Laurel had dropped him off, but she'd be out at the Bowdens' by the time he was done here. He knew the way home but didn't like the idea of walking home alone in the middle of the night, so he hoped he had enough money to get a Lyft.

The money from Yara had gone through and he breathed a little easier.

Maybe he'd even make a few tips. He hadn't expected that.

When the first person approached his table, he realized just how long it had been since he'd done a reading for someone other than his sister. His tongue clung to the roof of his mouth and when he licked his lips, they only felt sticky afterward.

He could do this and had done it a hundred times. He sucked in a breath and offered the cards to the person across from him.

Three people lingered off to one side and West decided that he'd stick with a three-card spread, a quick and easy past-present-future reading for everyone.

After four people, all of whom left a dollar in the tip cup, West eased up and no longer felt like he was forcing the situation. The cards moved more easily in his hands and he didn't have to struggle as much to interpret what they were trying to tell them.

It was no longer seeing the ace of pentacles and giving a vague interpretation but knowing that it meant that the young man across from him would likely be getting one of the jobs he'd applied to last week.

Time whisked by and a few times he had to go over to Yara to refresh his coffee or to ask her if he could change in all the singles from his tips for a few fives so they wouldn't keep spilling out of the cup.

She gave him the coffee and the fives with a laugh and a pat on the back. "Diana said you were good with your cards."

"Yeah, well, she's my mom, she's supposed to say nice things about me."

Yara laughed again.

Around midnight, the smell of cologne and cigarettes tickled his nose and he looked around immediately, scanning the room for the face he shouldn't have been able to recognize so readily.

His stomach didn't drop like it had at the craft fair. Instead, his chest swelled up with butterflies and he stammered his way through the rest of his current reading, continuing to steal glances across the coffee shop.

Kit saw him staring and smiled. He ambled over and sat across from West.

"So you're not gonna try to tell me you work here too," West said when he managed to unstick his tongue from the roof of his mouth.

"No. But I might have been out getting drinks with a few friends down the street and one of them might have mentioned that all you pointy-hat-and-broomstick types were having some kind of big holiday today."

West wondered what bar he'd come from; down the street, there was Blackrock, popular with locals but not exactly popular with the queer crowd and there was Tommy's, which was queer-friendly only in the sense that the unnatural creatures that lurked there didn't care about almost anything. West didn't care for either locale, but he could see Kit blending in at Tommy's. "That's not the whole truth."

From his back pocket, Kit produced a folded-up flyer advertising an alcohol-free celebration of Beltane with music, food, and free Tarot readings. "By Lowell Falls' own Westley Archer," Kit read, tapping the words beneath the picture of Tarot cards. "I didn't know you warranted introduction like that."

"No, uh, just. Yara likes to hire locally."

"I can kind of tell by the band," Kit said, his eyes sliding towards the blandly inoffensive music coming from the stage.

"And she's kind of dating my mom."

The demon chortled. He reached out and tapped the cards.

"So."

"It's free."

Kit pulled his hand back and shrugged, looking a little less blasé than he had a moment ago. "No, I've got a good enough idea of where my life's been."

"Chicken," West accused.

Kit met his eyes and held the gaze for a second. "Fine, then, go ahead."

West nodded towards the cards. "Give them a shuffle. Think about what you want to know. Have a question in mind."

It was almost funny to watch the demon hesitate as he reached for the cards. When his fingers finally closed around the deck, however, they did so with surety and he shuffled them the same way. West got the sense that Kit could have been an excellent liar if he put his mind to it.

The other man kept his eyes trained on West's hands as he dealt the cards and West had never been so aware of every hangnail, ripped cuticle, and knobby knuckle.

"What's your question?" West asked.

Kit shrugged. "Just general stuff I guess."

A lie. He had something specific he wanted to know but West wasn't about to interrogate the man over a Tarot reading.

West turned the first card. "This one's your past. Three of swords. Um, this one's about changing partners. Specifically divorce, I'm getting."

"You already knew that."

West pressed his lips together. "Doesn't make it less true."

"You pointy-hats—"

"You were the one asking for a divorce," West interrupted. "You guys were arguing a lot."

Kit rolled his eyes. "You already knew that, too."

"Arguing about another person, it feels like, someone who was important to both of you but...but in two different directions." West didn't delve any deeper, seeing that Kit had shifted a little in his seat and pulled his arms back. West flipped the second card. "Here's your present. More swords, gee. This one, the ace of swords, isn't...well." Normally this card didn't raise the hairs on the back of his neck, but tonight he didn't like this card, didn't like the way it sat with him.

"What?"

West shouldn't have goaded him into a reading. "It's...maybe it's seeing someone in a new light. In a way you won't really like but...it's also. It could be maybe some new animosity." *Enemy!* was the word blaring through his mind, but he didn't want to be an alarmist.

Kit said nothing, just sat there with his mouth drawn tight.

West flipped the last card. He let out a sigh, not aware until then that he had been holding his breath. "The Magician."

"That's...good?" Kit asked, his voice almost hushed.

"It's...it's a card of will. There's some problem-solving going on in your future," West told him. "And making connections so whatever it is that's over here..." He waved his hand towards the ace of swords. "It's going to work out, you know, it's going to work out if you can make it work out. It's saying...you've got the capability, so you'll need the will power to do it."

"That sounds better than divorce and animosity, at least."

Heat climbed from West's gut up his neck to his chest. "Yeah, I..."

"No, it's fine. I don't believe in that shit anyway."

A lie, but a tentative one. He didn't want to believe. Kit cleared his throat and rubbed his nose.

Other people had lined up behind him and West looked at the time. "I'm working until one."

The demon's eyes crawled over West's face and held West's gaze for a moment. "I should sober up before I try to drive anywhere anyway." He stood and headed over to the counter.

For the last half an hour, West kept looking towards the demon, sitting by himself, away from the witches, who skirted around him like he might pounce or be contagious.

As soon as he finished the last reading, West grabbed all his stuff and shoved it into his backpack. He took a few quick steps in the demon's direction then made himself slow down. He shouldn't have been this excited.

"Mind if I sit for a little while?" West asked him.

"Go ahead."

West sat. "You, uh, you go out a lot or was this, like, a special occasion?"

"Um. Some of my friends have been trying to get me to go out and it was one of their birthdays, so I, you know, I made my appearance," Kit explained.

"It was cool that you came by."

"Yeah, I'm surprised they let me in." He nodded his head

towards the barista, who was half-fairy and kept throwing Kit nasty glances. "I thought that one was about to have a heart attack when I walked over to the counter."

"You guys do kind of keep to yourselves."

Kit snorted. "Yeah, I guess that's one way of looking at it." He reached into his jacket, then stopped halfway. "I remember when people were allowed to smoke inside."

"Oh, there's...come on out back, there's a little space behind the building where Yara lets people smoke."

West stood and took a few steps towards the back of the building, glancing back to see if Kit had followed him.

He had.

Nerves bubbled in West's stomach in a way they hadn't in years.

Once outside and as Kit reached into his jacket, West couldn't help but say, "You know, those things will kill you."

"I'm not looking to live forever." He brought the cigarette to his lips but didn't light it. After another second, he pulled it away and jabbed a finger towards West. "You know, you never called or anything."

"What?" The accusation took West off-guard.

"I gave you my number."

"I didn't ask for it," West pointed out.

Kit sighed. "I mean...you *are*, aren't you?"

"Are what?" West asked, knowing what he meant but playing dumb anyway. He sort of liked seeing the other man flustered, even as minimal as Kit's unease was.

"Gay."

"No."

The demon's mouth popped open and he let out a nervous chuckle. He raked his hand through his hair. "I...I, uh, shit..." Panic flashed across his face, unadulterated for one second before it was covered up by him lighting his cigarette and drawing in a deep drag.

"I'm not gay, I'm pan," West said, wishing he hadn't made the other man worry like that. It was never easy to put yourself out there, straight or queer, and West had no idea what kind of acceptance Kit had gotten growing up.

Kit closed his mouth, opened it again, then let out an annoyed sigh and shaking his head.

West could only say, "They're different."

"Alright, well, that clears that up, then," Kit said.

"Does it? 'Cause I'm still kind of in the dark."

"You know, a guy gives you his number, it really only means one thing."

"That he still wants my help solving the murder of his ex-husband?" West guessed, though by now he'd worked out that it hadn't been Kit's intention.

"Or he thinks you're cute," the demon mumbled, his eyes trained on his boots. "But whatever, never mind about any of it."

He flicked his cigarette, only half-smoked, onto the pavement and ground it out. He glanced at West almost like he'd hoped West would be gone, then shoved both his hands into his pockets.

"Anyway, I guess...Well, I won't see you around," Kit said. "I can go around that way to get out front, right?" He jerked his head towards the mouth of the alley.

West closed his mouth and swallowed. He'd frozen awkwardly with his hands halfway between his face and his hips. He had lost any sense of what he should be doing with his limbs and thought it was lucky his legs hadn't gone haywire, too.

He smoothed out his shirt, not sure why he'd decided to worry about that, especially when Kit was still looking at him, his nose wrinkled a little now and his mouth quirked off to one side.

"You could see me," West said, able to feel his heartbeat through his whole body. "I mean..."

No, no, Kit couldn't see him. There was no way that things would ever work out between him and a demon who was twelve years his senior.

"You mean?" Kit prompted.

"I mean, uh, you know, like you're seeing me right now," he babbled.

And who said things had to work out? Kit had a messy life, as far as West could tell, but nothing had to be set in stone. It didn't have to be anything more than a one-time thing and West found that he badly wanted at least one time with Kit.

It didn't even have to go any closer to home than this alley or Kit's car.

His blood echoing in his ears, West moved in a little closer, not sure what would happen next.

Kit moved in too, his hands sliding around West's hips to pull him in and close the gap between their bodies.

West wondered if Kit could feel his heart pounding through his chest. This was the closest he had been to anyone in so long and he found himself winding his arms around the other man's neck and, when their lips finally met, West wanted to draw him in even closer.

He opened his mouth against Kit's and found the other man tasting of coffee and cigarettes in a way that should have been unpleasant. His tongue swept through West's mouth and when he pulled back for a breath, Kit drew him back in half a second, his whole body starting to warm.

He wanted more, though, and when Kit pushed against him, he let the other man back him up against the brick wall of the alley, the only sound that of their shoes scuffling against the pavement as they pushed and dragged each other.

In the back of his mind, something said that this was dangerous and stupid, hooking up with a stranger like this in some alley behind a coffee shop. He didn't care.

He forgot to worry altogether when Kit started to undo the drawstring of West's joggers, fumbling with the knot. When he couldn't get right away, he slid his palm against the hard length of West's cock through the thin fabric of the pants, making West grunt and thrust against his hand. When Kit squeezed a little harder, West caught his mouth again, grinding against Kit's hand and biting the demon's lip.

It had been too goddamn long.

Kit's phone started to ring, the tone jangling, unnervingly loud. He pulled back and West held onto him.

"Don't," West begged, "Just ignore it."

"I can't." Kit pulled back, no longer interested in what West had to offer at all. "I can't, it's my sitter."

West tried to untangle the meaning of that as Kit brought the phone to his ear. "Hello?"

His sitter?

The demon had his phone clenched in his hand so tight that his knuckles had gone pale. "What do you mean he...? Yeah, I know, he does that, I told you...We *talked* about that, did you follow the notes?" Kit raked a hand through his hair and sighed. Through the phone, West could sort of make out the worried voice of a teenage girl and the screaming of a child. "For Christ's sakes, Becky, he's *four*, don't try to argue with him!" He sighed again, somewhere between disgusted and pissed. When he spoke again, though, his voice had a softer tone. "No, no, I'm coming back."

Kit hung up and looked at West. "I...Listen, I've got to go."

West nodded. "Everything alright?"

"He's just been having a hard time sleeping, his schedule's been off ever since..."

"No, it's fine."

He took a step towards the door, his eyes on West's face, on his mouth. "Maybe..."

"Listen, if you need to go, then go."

Kit offered his phone to West and requested, "Your number?" hopeful but tentative, as though he wasn't sure if West would give it to him.

The headiness of their closeness had faded, leaving West with the taste of cigarettes in his mouth and an odd feeling of shame and disorientation. He sighed with disgust, but took Kit's phone anyway and put in his number.

His actual number, even though he'd thought about putting in a fake one. With a pissed-off huff, feeling spoiled and petty, he returned the phone to Kit's hand.

He had no reason to be a brat about this.

Except that he hadn't felt this way in so long and he was still aching, wanting Kit to kiss him again. The only thing that stayed his hand was having to contend with the cold splash of water that had been finding out that Kit had a son.

"So. You're...you've got a kid, though?"

The demon nodded. "Yeah. Riley. Anyway, I have to go, he was having a hard time."

"Sure, yeah."

Kit took one step, then doubled back to kiss West one last time. After the kiss broke, Kit licked his lips, then hurried away, stalking back through the coffee shop like a man who had to go save the world.

West gathered up all his things, called a Lyft, and when he was home, he stripped down, hoping that getting rid of the clothes would get rid of the smell Kit had left on him.

It hadn't.

The cologne, the smoke, clung to him, to his very skin and made him think of things that should have been left alone.

He couldn't sleep and tried to blame it on all the free coffee. Eventually, he had to admit that too much caffeine wasn't the source of his restlessness.

It was memories of a tongue in his mouth, a hand on his cock, a body pressing him up against the wall. He couldn't get the thought of the other man from his mind and, soon enough, that had him slipping his hand between his own legs, imagining that it was Kit's hand sliding over him. It was only after he came that he was reasonably clear-headed again and remembered how bad of an idea it would be to get involved with a chain-smoking demon who was not just twelve years his senior but also a single father.

They didn't *have* to get involved, he reminded himself. There was nothing about copping a feel in an alleyway that indicated Kit expected anything more than something casual. Very casual. It could still be just a one-time thing. It would be *best* if it was just a one-time thing.

Now they'd just have to arrange some other time.

May 1
Sunday

WEST WOKE up to an empty house and a badly mangled text from his sister telling him that she was sleeping at the Bowdens'. She'd sent it at five in the morning, so he figured he wouldn't be seeing her until sometime in the late afternoon.

It wasn't the text he'd been hoping for, though.

He jogged, showered, and ate his breakfast, checking his phone as though it was keeping secrets from him.

He let Mipsy have the run of the house while he cleaned her hutch. Normally, that job fell to Laurel, as it was her rabbit, but he didn't think she was going to be in any shape to do much more than sit on the couch and veg out when she came home.

His hoodie from yesterday smelled like cigarettes and he knew he should wash it to get the stink out. Something stayed him from tossing it in with the other laundry when he went to put in a load.

He brought the sweatshirt to his nose and inhaled, catching the scent of cologne beneath the stench of smoke. The smell alone made his stomach quiver.

Nothing more than basic animal attraction. Something West needed to get out of his system. Kit was decent-looking and he had an easy confidence about him.

Except for those few instances when panic had flashed across his face the other night.

West's heart tightened at the memory.

He shoved the sweatshirt into the washing machine and slammed it closed.

This was stupid.

He didn't let himself think about it for too long. He didn't let himself think about it at all, really. He cleaned the entire house, top to bottom. Once he'd physically cleaned the house, he threw open the windows and did a spiritual cleanse as well.

He'd spent enough time lingering in the mindset of someone who had gotten dumped, someone who'd lost their job.

He was going to...do something, certainly. What exactly it was that he needed to do wasn't clear.

He closed the windows, wrapped himself up in a blanket, and hunkered down on the couch, all the will and good intentions draining out of him in the face of a little uncertainty. He settled in for a four-hour marathon of daytime cooking shows.

Around five in the evening, Laurel shuffled in.

He took one look at her and pronounced, "Oof."

She grunted. "Shut up, Westley."

"You want me to make you some tea?"

"I've had tea," she told him. "I've had enough tea to put England to shame."

"You, uh, you want something stronger than tea?"

"I need to sleep." She didn't go to her room, though, but collapsed next to him on the couch.

"Did you have fun, at least?"

"I had a blast. From what I remember."

He didn't bother to call her out on her lie. She was allowed to have a bad time at a party without him giving her the fourth degree. He pulled down the other blanket from the back of the couch and spread it out over her. She kicked off her shoes and burrowed into the couch.

"What about you?" she asked, "How was the Knot?"

"Fine." His heart sped up. "I didn't make anyone cry."

"Oh, that's good."

He tightened the blanket around his shoulders.

He thought she'd fallen asleep when she stayed quiet, but eventually, she glanced at him and asked, "Hey, did you ever hear back from Leia?"

He swallowed. "I think she said she had some stuff to take care of."

"Mmm. You guys would be a cute couple."

He hummed noncommittally and handed her the remote. "Here, you find something to watch. You want something to eat? I'm getting up."

"Maybe some toast. If you don't mind."

He didn't mind at all.

From the kitchen, the blanket still wrapped around his shoulders, he made her toast and decided he would make himself some soup. He heard his phone ding in the other room and his hand clenched around the handle of the pot he'd grabbed to heat up the soup.

He set down the pot and went to pull the lid off the soup.

"Who's texting you, is this Leia's number?" Laurel called.

He yanked the lid off the soup so hard it sloshed over his hand. He rushed to wipe his hand and practically ran into the living room. He snatched his phone out of her hand.

"Hey!" she cried.

"Don't *hey* me, don't read my texts," he snapped.

He retreated back into the kitchen, swiping anxiously at the screen to see what Kit had texted him.

Hey sorry I had to cut and run like that last night.

West scowled at the message, thinking that Kit could have bothered to send him a message earlier in the day. He immediately chided himself for thinking like that. He didn't have any intention to get touchy-feely about any of this.

He sent out a reply. *Whatever it's fine. u clearly were needed elsewhere.*

West shoved his phone into his pocket and hovered over his soup, waiting for it to heat up and definitely not waiting for Kit to text him back.

When the response did come, West grabbed his phone as soon as the text appeared on the screen. *Anyway maybe we could get together some time to talk.*

To talk? What the hell did they have to talk about? Talk had to be a euphemism for 'finish what we started.'

Another message from Kit came a second later. *And also I kind of wanted to ask you for a favor.*

That rang true, but he had no idea what kind of favor Kit would want from him. Probably something else to do with his dead ex-husband. His heart crawled up his throat as he wrote a message to send back. *What kind of favor?*

West's soup started to bubble and he took it off the stove, pouring it carefully into a mug and dropping off Laurel's toast with her on the couch.

He took his soup and his phone, angling towards the basement.

"Where are you going?" his sister asked.

He ignored her, making the trek down the stairs slowly to avoid getting soup everywhere. He settled onto the futon in the corner, his eyes turned towards the small TV he had down there. He didn't have a cable hookup down here, but he did have a Blu-ray player and a collection of well-loved movies. He threw in the first movie he put his hands on, a copy of *A Walk in the Sun* that his grandfather had given him.

West needed something familiar right now and a three-hour black-and-white film that he pretty much knew by heart would be just the thing to soothe his nerves. The opening scene alone conjured the plush, yellow couch of his grandparents' living room where he'd spent so many childhood afternoons, resting his head against his grandfather's arm as they watched war movies or reruns of MASH.

When Kit finally texted him back, West had calmed considerably. *I need to go to Mike's apartment to pick something up and I don't want to have to go alone.*

Feeling callous, West needed to ask *u don't have any friends u can ask?*

Friends that all knew Mike. I don't know I thought maybe you'd be more neutral about it than they would. If you don't want to don't worry about it.

Something ran a little false about the words, but West figured it was because Kit had other motives than thinking West would be more neutral or maybe because there was no way that all of his friends had known Mike. In any event, West didn't have much interest in accompanying anyone to the scene of a violent death and he was set to refuse when he received another message.

I know it really is weird. Weirder than waiting around on your porch for you to ask you questions about my dead ex but I don't know who else to ask and I think if I have to go alone I might lose it.

That was true.

It was more than true, it was unguarded, and it nipped West's refusal in the bud. He stared at the text for a while, not sure what to do. He set the phone down and trained his eyes on the TV, the mug of soup clasped between his hands. He took a few sips of soup and thought about the way Kit's nonchalant mask had slipped a few times that night. He thought what it must have been like to be in his shoes, dealing with whatever it was he had to deal with, the dead ex and the kid included.

He picked up his phone and replied with *ok what time.*

Kit arranged to come by in the late morning the following day after he'd dropped his son off at preschool and Laurel had left for work. West had absolutely no desire to see how any interaction between his sister and the demon would go.

Once they'd made their arrangement, West let the conversation peter out.

No.

He let it die. There was no gentle winding down, he just replied with one-word answers until Kit stopped texting back.

When he went upstairs to put the mug in the dishwasher, he found Laurel still on the couch, snoring like a bear.

He went over to nudge her awake and noticed that she had tear streaks down her face. He gave her a gentle shake.

"Hmm? What?"

"Laurel, is everything alright?" he asked, sitting at the end of the couch. He put a hand on her leg.

"Yeah. Fine."

He accused, "Liar."

She rubbed her face. "No, it's just, you know. Richard was there."

He should have known that Richard would be the source of her distress. He had been for decades, at this point. "And? Richard knows the Bowdens, too, you must have figured you'd see him."

"His wife is pregnant."

West held in the groan and eye roll that made up his immediate response. He didn't know why he bothered to ask her about her problems anymore. "You need to find something else to focus all this energy on."

She glared. "Like what?" she growled.

"I don't know. Join a gym maybe and work out all this rage instead of directing it at me." He stood and went into the kitchen, loading dirty dishes into the dishwasher so he would have a reason not to go back into the living room.

He should have been a good brother, offered her a shoulder to cry on, except that he'd started to find her infatuation with Richard irritating and pathetic instead of sympathetic. It wasn't anyone's fault that they weren't together; it certainly wasn't Richard's wife's fault, though Laurel liked to talk about how Katrina 'just wasn't right' for Richard.

Laurel followed him into the kitchen, the blanket wrapped around her shoulders. She put her plate in the dishwasher. "She's not right for him."

He groaned. "Laurel."

"What?" she demanded. "She isn't. He's my *best friend*, alright? I can tell that—"

"So if she's not right for him they'll get divorced or something. Whatever's gonna happen between them will happen. You should worry about *not* spending all your energy wishing her ill. She's never done anything to you—"

"She—"

He cut her off, "Except have the balls to ask out the guy you *didn't* have the balls to ask out."

Instead of looking angry, Laurel's face crumpled.

Immediately, West tried to backpedal, softening his tone and advising, "Listen. You've got to worry about *you*. Good things don't come to people who don't let them."

"What's that even supposed to mean?"

"It means that maybe you're not right for Richard either. Maybe he's not right for you and worrying about him is keeping you from getting to where you're supposed to be." He closed the dishwasher and wiped his hands on his pants. "So try, at least, to find something else. Go out and meet people, huh? You never know."

"Nice coming from you," she huffed.

He didn't argue, knowing it would be pointless. Laurel didn't understand that he wasn't looking to get set up on dates. It wasn't that he didn't want to meet anyone, but his sister combing through every eligible match in the area wasn't exactly his idea of romance.

He headed back to his room after that; the air needed to clear between the two of them and he needed to find something else to think about.

May 2
Monday

TEN O'CLOCK was too late. Laurel had left at eight-thirty and West found himself wishing that he'd told Kit to come over at eight-thirty-five.

Not because he was so desperate to see the demon but because he hated to wait.

His unease had nothing to do with the smell of cologne buried under cigarettes or the feel of a leather jacket in his hands as he fervently pulled a body closer to his and definitely not the sensation of being palmed through his joggers.

No, definitely not.

He found himself considering sending a text to Kit to let him know that he could come over early if he had nowhere else to be.

He thought about it a lot, but never actually followed through.

Instead, he spent the hour and a half doing meal prep for the week, carefully measuring out portions of salmon, asparagus, and cherry tomatoes. Four hundred and fifty calories each. By Thursday, he'd be sniffing around whatever carb-and-fat laden meal Laurel had made herself for dinner, but his will would hold out. It had for a while now and he took too much pride in that, but it was about the only thing he could count as an accomplishment.

Westley Archer: that guy who sure could stick to a diet. Better than Westley Archer: that unemployed guy who lives with his sister.

He sighed as he closed the fridge and jumped when the doorbell rang.

When he pulled open the door, the sight of Kit didn't bring butterflies, arousal, or even mild nausea, all of which West had sort of anticipated. Instead, the first thing that came to mind was that he had jerked off and imagined Kit doing it for him.

He stared at Kit, trying to form any coherent thought that didn't involve masturbating. His face grew hot and he hoped his cheeks hadn't gone red. "Hey."

"Hi."

The demon seemed just as uncomfortable as West; he stood about a foot back from the door and had his hands shoved into his pockets.

"You want to come in?" West asked.

The demon gave a small shake of his head. "I've got to meet Jess there at ten-thirty."

"Oh." West checked for his keys, wallet, and phone then stepped out of the house. As he locked the door, he asked, "Who's Jess?"

"Mike's sister. She's got the keys."

"Oh." West wished he had something better to say.

After they had gotten in the car, Kit added, "She also thinks I had something to do with Mike being dead. Like...I don't know if she's ready to directly accuse me of cold-blooded murder but...well, she never liked me anyway."

"Was your divorce that bad?"

"The divorce was only the half of it," Kit admitted. "Custody battles. They're not pretty."

West pulled at a loose hangnail and regretted it when it started to bleed. He sucked at his finger for a second then said, lamely, "So you've got a kid."

Kit let out a small laugh. "Yeah. I do. I think we went over this already."

"I just, well, I didn't figure you for a dad."

"Most people don't," Kit told him and West caught the edge in his voice. Barely there but there all the same.

"Is..." West trailed off, thinking that it wasn't any of his business.

"What?"

"Your ex, you were having custody issues? I mean, like...what kind of custody issues?" he asked, wondering if Kit might have some kind of problem that had gotten his custody rights reduced or revoked.

"I only had him on weekends. It used to be more when he was younger especially 'cause I don't work during the day. It worked out really well. Then Mike got him into this preschool last year and I didn't want him to go. Mike basically made it seem like...like it was negligent of me when I wasn't sending him and it was this whole fucking to-do and..." Kit let out a sigh. "Anyway, Riley was biologically Mike's, and you put that together with...Listen to me go, you don't want to hear any of this."

"I asked," West pointed out.

Kit glanced towards him. "Yeah."

"So you put it together with...?" West prompted.

"With a guy like me." He rolled his eyes. "Whatever. I get it. No one looks at me and thinks, gee *he* looks like he'd be a great dad."

West didn't have any comfort to offer, especially when he agreed with people. Kit didn't look like he'd be a good dad and West wasn't even convinced that the other man was a good father. He barely knew him.

They sat quietly for a while.

"Explains why your car smells like applesauce," West mentioned after a few more minutes.

Kit glanced his way and then grinned.

"I thought it was really weird!" West explained, a smile spreading across his face, too. "Like, oh, here's this chain-smoking demon who just, I don't know, *loves* applesauce."

"I think the kid would bathe in the stuff if I let him."

Inside the car, Kit remained more at ease, but once they parked and headed into the building, something about his demeanor changed. He produced a pack of cigarettes and brought one to his lips before West had time to register the movement, or to lodge a protest.

"I thought you were quitting."

West swiveled his head to the left to see that the voice belonged to a forty-something woman walking towards them. She wore heels that clicked firmly as she moved in their direction and had the same clean-cut look as Mike; West could only assume this was Jess and, judging by the look on her face, he didn't think they'd be doing introductions.

Kit barely looked her way. He grunted noncommittally in the woman's direction and West got the feeling Kit would have stood there smoking and throwing the butts at her feet if he could have.

"Are we going inside or what?" she asked.

That got the demon's attention a little better. "I was kind of hoping you'd just give me the key."

"Why? So you can case the joint?" she sneered.

"Rob," Kit corrected. "I could still case it if you came in."

He took a final drag and tossed the butt on the ground. He made no move to pick it up.

"Those are toxic, you know," West pointed out.

"Yeah, I know," the demon replied with a sour look and an eye roll. "Consider me well versed in the dangers of smoking and then don't ever mention it again."

West added, "Toxic for the environment."

"What?"

"Yeah, when you leave them lying around like that all the shit inside them leeches out into the environment."

Kit looked to the butt he'd left smoldering on the pavement. When a huff, he scooped it up and deposited it in the nearest trash. He asked the woman, "So can I have the key or not?"

Instead of answering him, she set off towards the apartment building. Kit followed her, grumbling under his breath, and West followed behind, wishing he'd stayed home. Kit didn't need him here.

Once on the third floor, Jess unlocked the apartment door and stepped inside first. She crossed her arms and blocked most of the threshold. Kit had to squeeze past her to get through the door and West edged in after him, not knowing if it would be better to linger in the hall or follow him in.

The air inside the apartment had an odd smell to it. Cleaning products and the smell that spaces got when they'd been closed up too long, not quite musty, but something similar. He wanted to open the windows and light some candles.

"You've got five minutes," Jess told him.

Kit glanced her way, his eyes hard and flat. His lips were pressed into a thin line and he basically stalked through the living room towards the hallway.

Watching him move like that reminded West why it was best to stay away from demons. Even dilute as he was, he'd be able to do a lot of damage in a fight and that was without even considering what kind of magic he might be able to call up.

West glanced at Jess, then headed after Kit, edging around the clean lines of the beige couch and white area rug. The whole place was tidy. More than tidy. It was orderly, in a rigid way that made it hard to imagine this place ever being home to Kit or a four-year-old.

And it was spotless. West couldn't tell where the murder had taken place and the idea that he might have been treading over the place where someone had taken his last breaths sat uneasily in his gut.

He found Kit standing inside a bedroom painted a tasteful steel blue. One wall bore a hand-painted mural of round-bodied sea life with large eyes; it looked like a scene out of a picture book. Up against this wall was a small bed, rumpled like someone had slept in it last night.

An awful idea dawned on West. "Kit."

The demon glanced in West's direction, one eyebrow raised.

"He didn't...I mean, was your son home when...?"

"No. Thank Christ, no. He was with a neighbor. Mike got him up in the middle of the night and dropped him off a few doors down."

"So he knew someone was coming over."

"Yeah, that's the consensus." Kit surveyed the room again. "It's, uh, it's this stuffed rabbit, about this big." He showed a span of about eight inches with his hands. "Help me look, will you?"

"Sure."

While they were looking, Kit found an overnight bag and stuffed it with clothes and a few other toys.

The room was surprisingly free of clutter. The few toys and books that West could see were all neatly shelved; it was a far cry from how he remembered his room being as a child.

West went to search beneath the bed and Kit went to the closet, still rifling through clothes and shoving some of them in the bag after he'd checked the tags.

West pulled out his phone and used the light to get a better view of the floor under the bed. He didn't see a stuffed rabbit, but there were a few other things scattered under there. He fished them out and double-checked for the rabbit.

A few puzzle pieces and a sock.

"Would it be anywhere else? In the living room or something?"

Kit glanced over and seemed a little disoriented by the

question. "What?"

"I mean...I left things all over when I was a kid. Maybe it's in another room?"

Kit shook his head, but it didn't seem to be a negation. "I don't know. Maybe. Mike was..."

"Tidy?"

"Yeah, that's one word for it," Kit agreed and sounded like he had a stronger word on the tip of his tongue.

"You want me to go look around?"

"Thanks."

West headed out into the apartment, moving further down the hall. A cursory glance in the bathroom revealed nothing.

The other room had to be Mike's bedroom. It felt sacrilegious to go in, but he turned the knob anyway. Within he found the same muted pallet and military-like neatness. Even the desk, which had been piled with papers, had things carefully stacked and sorted.

The bed was made, which reinforced the idea that Mike had known someone was coming over the night of his death. This hadn't been some night-time intrusion, a burglary gone wrong or some domestic fight between lovers turned ugly. Nothing about the room suggested that Mike had a boyfriend, or if he did, not the kind of boyfriend that would keep his things here.

West stepped further into the room, the hair on the back of his neck standing up and his entire body tightening. He felt like any minute someone was about to come up behind him and stab him in the back.

He glanced back, terrified of what he would see and not knowing what he would even do to defend himself.

There was nothing.

He sucked in a deep breath and poked around the room a little. The rabbit wasn't anywhere to be found in the closet. West found suits and dress shoes on one side, and then more casual wear on the other, hiking boots and rugged clothes that made West think of hunting and gun ranges.

The desk, on closer inspection, had three piles. Finances, work, and then a weird collection of graphs and other sheets of paper covered in pluses and minuses all in carefully labeled manila file folders. Knowing it was none of his business, West rummaged through the papers, finding charts that recorded things like SIB and AGG. He kept going through them, not able to fully understand them. So many of the terms were foreign to him, in the sense that they were comprised of English words he understood but not in this context.

At the top was a letter saying that Mike had been invited to a PPT, whatever that was, at the start of May. Mike had rescheduled it for some day in June, apparently. Not that it mattered either way; Mike wouldn't be going to any meetings.

"Ahh, you found the Riley Files," Kit said from the doorway.

West screeched, jumped, and dropped the folder. The papers went flying, skating across the hardwood floor. He clenched his hands and squeezed his eyes shut, not sure what else to do.

Kit bit his lip but didn't laugh. "Sorry, sorry, I...I didn't mean to sneak up on you," he assured. "You were pretty absorbed."

West dropped to his knees and gathered up all the papers, shuffling them back into a stack. "I'm sorry, I wasn't, I shouldn't have been—"

"It's fine." Kit took the folder from West when he offered it and tossed it back onto the desk with little regard for the piles. "It's all garbage anyway." He gave the papers another glance. "Well. Not all of it. A lot of it," he amended.

"What is it?"

"It's all the data from Riley's preschool."

"Data?" West asked, knowing he shouldn't be pressing his luck or asking questions about things that were none of his business.

"Yeah, they have some twenty-something girl following him around all day and tallying how many times he scripts or jiggles his hands." Kit let out a sigh. "Like I said, most of it is garbage. But it's not the school's fault, you know? A lot of it was Mike thinking that he could, you know, control Riley like he could control everything else. I've got to talk to them about changing his goals..."

West looked back towards the folders. "Is."

Kit waited.

"It's none of my business, never mind." West stepped away from the desk and glanced around the room.

"He's got autism," Kit offered, no hint of hesitation in his voice.

West saw a paper that had skittered all the way to the other side of the room. He went over to pick it up and returned it to the desk. "I didn't see the rabbit."

Kit crossed the room and checked the bedside table. He pulled out a gray stuffed rabbit and it struck West as an odd place to keep a stuffed animal. "Big boys don't need bunnies to go to sleep," Kit said by way of explanation. " 'Cause, you know, a four-year-old is a big kid."

He added the rabbit to one of the bags he'd gotten together, its floppy ears poking out the top.

"I still have a stuffy in my room," West offered quietly.

"Yeah, well, Mike was...Mike went through a lot of shit when he was a kid and he did the whole military thing so, you know, I thought he needs his space, likes his privacy, likes to have certain things his way, no big deal, right? Turns out when it comes to having kids that kind of thing isn't just a big deal, it's a red flag."

West didn't think Kit should be telling him any of this. He didn't want to know any of it, not about his ex or his kid, he had no interest in knowing anything about Kit's life. Except here he was, not just listening but staring at the demon, checking his face for signs of that cool confidence slipping away.

And it was. His mouth was drawn tight, as it had been since the moment they'd arrived, but his eyes were now puffy and red-rimmed.

"I always tried to tell him that Riley...he needs time to do things his way, when he's ready but Mike was all about those developmental milestones. Didn't believe in baby steps, not even for kids." Kit pressed the back of his hand to his nose and drew in a breath. "How bad do I look?"

"Just a little...flushed."

"Alright, well, we ought to get out of here before Jess has a conniption." Kit handed over one of the bags to West. "I'll be out in a second."

West took the bag and headed into the living room. He heard the faucet running in the bathroom.

Jess had moved from the doorway to the kitchen but looked just as displeased as she had before.

When Kit emerged, no longer looking the least bit upset, she demanded, "You're taking *all* of that?"

"Yes? I thought it might be a good idea to have more than three changes of clothes for the kid," he told her.

She held out her hand. "Let me see it."

"What?"

"Give me those bags, I want to make sure you're not taking anything else," she said.

Kit closed his eyes for a moment and took in a deep breath, then handed the bag over to her. He took the one West had and plunked that one at her feet.

While she rifled through the bags, Kit wandered the living room, looking at the pictures hung on the wall. West waited by the doorway, watching Jess but trying not to be too obvious about it. She inspected each tiny shirt and pair of pants, shaking them all out like Kit might have been smuggling something.

She looked up and caught him staring, so he turned his eyes away, his gaze skating over the room.

Hanging against one of the windows was a suncatcher. Not only did it clash with the colors and design of the room, the bits of colored glass formed a spiky, angular symbol that West didn't know but he would have bet was supposed to have some kind of occult connection. It lacked the flowing calligraphy of the runes that mages used, though, and he didn't immediately recognize it, which meant it probably didn't have anything to do with common witchcraft, either.

He continued to look around the room and saw nothing else that seemed to go along with the suncatcher, nothing that was a similar style or color, nothing that made him think that this belonged in the apartment.

He tapped Kit on the arm and nodded towards the window.

The corners of the demon's mouth tugged down and he moved in towards the window, reaching up to touch it.

It clinked against the window and Jess's head snapped up from repacking the first bag. "What are you doing?" she demanded.

Kit pointed to the suncatcher. "I've never seen this before."

"You haven't lived here for two-and-a-half years," she reminded none too kindly.

"I was actually allowed inside the apartment from time to time. You know, to pick up my kid."

"And letting you near Riley was the biggest mistake Mike ever made, next to getting involved with you in the first place," she hissed.

"Really? I would have thought it was one of the times he got black-out drunk and locked himself in the bathroom with a gun. That would have been on my list of Mike's Top Ten Biggest Mistakes," Kit said, his voice even.

For now. West could see Kit's composure slipping, his breathing coming hard through his nose as he waited for Jess to say something back.

Instead of waiting for her reply, Kit went over and took the bags. She hadn't gone through the second one yet, but he took that too and headed out the door. He walked out of the apartment and she followed after him, shouting about how he had no right to talk about Mike like that.

West took the opportunity to unhook the suncatcher and slip it into the front pocket of his hoodie.

When Jess came back in and demanded, "What are you still doing here?" West said nothing and ran after Kit, catching up with him on the second floor.

KIT DIDN'T say a word, not until he'd stowed the bags in the trunk and both of them had gotten into the car.

"Let me buy you lunch," Kit offered without warning as he pulled out of the parking lot and headed down the street.

Caught by surprise, West answered, "No, uh. That's alright."

"Please. You didn't need to come out here with me and I...I know it was weird but it really did help to have you around. Lunch is the least I can do."

West shook his head. He hadn't done anything helpful. He assured Kit, "It's fine, you don't need to—"

"I need an excuse to be around another person right now."

The statement was more than just true, it was almost pleading. "It's not even lunchtime," West pointed out. "Why don't you...bring me home and you can come in. I'll...I'll make some tea or something."

Kit nodded.

The ride back was wordless, the only sound in the whole car was more of Kit's haunted, discordant music.

When Kit pulled into the driveway, he didn't turn off the car. "Listen, um...I don't have to come in. It's fine."

Smart idea. Kit, it seemed, had come to his senses about this. West, though, had done the opposite, and said, "Come inside."

Kit shook his head.

West wouldn't have felt right leaving him alone. He didn't know what Kit had to go home to and didn't think that sitting home by himself would do him any good. "Yeah, come on, I've got weed if you don't want tea."

The demon's head jerked up and he fixed West with a surprisingly wide-eyed look, as though no one had ever offered him weed before. "I...I can't." He sounded surprised with himself. "Mike's parents are trying to get custody of Riley."

"Just tea then."

Kit nodded and followed West inside.

"Do you think they have a shot?" West asked as he turned on the electric kettle.

"I don't think so. I hope not, anyway, but I'd rather not risk it. They've got biology *and* it was in Mike's will—"

"He had a will?" West asked, surprised that anyone in their forties had planned that far ahead. He didn't even think his mother had a will in order yet.

"He was anal like that," Kit said. "He put it in his will that he wanted Riley to go to his parents if anything happened to him. But, uh, my lawyer says children aren't property, so you can't bequeath them to anyone and that even though I'm not his biological father, I am still legally his parent."

"Better not to do anything risky, I guess," West agreed. "Some other time."

A small smile appeared on Kit's face, then grew into something sort of goofy and disbelieving. "If you say so."

West suddenly felt stupid, giving this man a standing invitation to come get high with him. That was much different from the one-time hookup West had decided on. He turned away from Kit and rummaged around in the cabinets for mugs, taking longer than he really needed.

Something in his pocket clacked against the counter and he took out the suncatcher.

"What's that?" Kit asked.

West turned around, his cheeks warm as he presented the suncatcher. "I, uh. I might have taken it."

"Stealing stuff and peddling narcotics?" Kit pretended to be scandalized.

"It's...I'm not..." West wanted to protest but couldn't think of any arguments. Finally, lamely, he pointed out, "It would only be peddling if I charged you."

The demon snorted and held out his hand.

West gave him the suncatcher.

"Do you know what this is?"

"No idea," West admitted. "But, you know, it just...it looked wrong in there. I don't think he picked it up in a gift shop."

"No, me neither." Kit set the suncatcher on the table and leaned back in his chair. He ran his fingers through his hair. "Thanks, though. For coming with me."

West shrugged. "You didn't seem like you were going to lose it or anything."

"Yeah, well," Kit said and didn't elaborate.

The kettle came to a boil and West was glad for an excuse to do something with his hands. He brought the tea over to the table and stared down into his mug.

After a minute, Kit cleared his throat.

West looked up. "Hmm?"

"No, uh...and I can't think of any good way to transition into this, so I guess..." Kit shrugged and scrubbed one hand over his cheek. "Just about the other night."

"Oh."

"Yeah. Just. I get it. The whole thing is just...inappropriate."

West frowned. That hadn't been the word he'd been expecting. "What do you mean?"

"I mean here I am showing up at your house and giving you my number and stalking you to coffee shops in the middle of the night and...I understand that this is one hundred percent insane on my part, but I...I'm at a loss here, really. I don't know what else to do."

"No, it's...you're making it sound a lot worse than it is," West assured. "I don't even feel a little bit stalked."

Kit shook his head. "Still. I feel nuts."

"I guess from now on you can just text me instead of showing up at my house, then," West offered, not realizing for a few seconds that 'from now on' had the implication that they'd see each other again.

"What if I called you?"

"I definitely would not answer the phone, who the hell makes phone calls anymore?" West asked, ladling on as much mock-disgust as he could.

He got a smile for his trouble.

"Besides," West said after a short bout of silence. "I wasn't even mad that you showed up at the Knot."

"No?"

"No, I, uh...I kind of figured we could, you know, finish what we started."

Kit let out a low whistle. "Stealing things, giving away drugs, *and* hooking up with a stranger? Shit, you witches get up to a lot more than anyone ever lets on."

"You're not exactly a *stranger*." True, he couldn't think of Kit's last name off the top of his head, but he had learned too much about him to consider the demon a stranger anymore.

"Yeah, you're right, you've been in my car twice."

"And all I did was steal something. I didn't give you anything and we haven't even hooked up yet," West pointed out, not sure why he felt the need to defend himself.

"Yet," Kit echoed. "Is this how you normally pick up guys? Invite them in for tea? Folks at the senior center have got to be worried about competing with you."

There was a segue there, somewhere, and West knew that if he played things right he could get Kit out of his clothes and into bed before it was even lunchtime.

Part of him wanted it, thinking of the warmth of Kit's mouth, the firmness of his grip, recalling all the things he had imagined them doing together and how badly he had wanted to make them a reality.

A larger, or at least more vocal part, balked at the idea. It felt wrong, somehow, knowing that Kit had been close to tears in that apartment. That he was probably still feeling out of sorts now, too, no matter how even he kept his features or his voice.

West was hesitant to think of the demon as vulnerable but pursuing him now would have felt like taking advantage. He took a sip of tea and adjusted his grip on the mug, trying to figure out how he felt about all of this. "What'd you do to make that woman hate you so much?"

The demon's eyes popped open and his head jerked up.

"And, I mean, if the grandparents want custody..." West trailed off with a shrug. "I mean, is it just a gay thing?"

Kit smirked. "No, not really."

West raised his eyebrows expectantly.

"I made some stupid choices when I was a kid and I guess it's hard for people to believe that I'm not like that anymore. I mean, they never liked me, really, but I think they were more alright with things when we were just dating. The more serious our relationship got, the more Mike's family liked to point out that I..." Kit trailed off. "Well, you know, I've got a few misdemeanors under my belt and they really didn't appreciate that."

"What kind of misdemeanors?"

"Disorderly conduct, disruption of a funeral, patronizing a prostitute," the demon listed cheerily. "It's actually kind of a miracle I never got busted for possession..." He trailed off with a far-away look on his face; West guessed that he must have been recounting all the close calls.

"Wow."

"Yeah, nineteen ninety-five through two thousand one was a wild ride," Kit admitted. "But that was...you know, that was then. I'm, uh, you know, I'm...what's the word? Reformed, I guess."

West sipped his tea, not sure what to say. He'd been in first grade in nineteen ninety-five, but that didn't seem like a worthy addition to the conversation. Instead, he said, "Recovered."

"Right, recovered." Kit cleared his throat and started to talk, his words sort of running together, "The one about the prostitute is, well, it's, actually a funny story, 'cause she *was* a prostitute but I was just trying to buy some coke. I let them think I was soliciting 'cause that's only a misdemeanor and I don't have a lot of interest in being a felon. And that's the story of how I came out to my mom as gay *and* a drug addict."

"How'd that go?"

"She was...really good about it. Both parts. Sent me to rehab," Kit said with a small smile. "For drugs, thank god, not the other way around. She's pretty much a saint."

West ripped at a hangnail. Everything Kit had shared had been true, tinged more with omission than dishonesty.

"Ouch," Kit commented.

West looked up.

The demon nodded towards the blood welling up around West's cuticle. "That looks like it hurts."

It stung, certainly. "It's fine." He sucked the blood away. "Bad habit," he said, his mouth filled with the taste of iron. Almost as soon as he took his finger from his mouth, the blood returned.

Kit's hand moved towards his, his fingers half-curled as though he were going to close his hand around West's. "I can, uh, I can take care of that."

West quickly drew his hand back, bringing it close to his chest. He didn't think Kit meant to do him any harm, but if Kit was offering what West thought he was, he didn't want any part in it. Witches and mages might have worked magic in different ways, but they were both beholden to a set of rules and hierarchies. Creatures like demons weren't bound by any kind of principles and they didn't need spells to work their magic; their power was innate and limited only by their imaginations and the inborn potency of their abilities. For the first handful of generations, Devil spawn were deeply hazardous things to be around.

There was no polite way to turn down an offer like Kit's.

Most witches wouldn't have worried about being polite about it.

West never got the chance to think of a gracious decline. He'd spent too long staring at Kit's hand in abject horror.

The demon pulled back. "Sorry. Unclean. I forgot that we like to keep our devilry separate from our witchcraft."

"Kit..."

"No, I get it, I do. After all, I'm descended from the Dark Lord himself," Kit conceded. "You just work for him."

"I...!" West crossed his arms. "I don't *work* for him."

"Then how'd you get mixed up in this? There's not a lot of ways to get those black coins and even less that are, umm, decent."

"How'd you get yours?" West asked.

"Stole it," Kit answered casually.

True. That worried West a little, but he didn't have too much time to fret about it because Kit pressed, "So, really, how'd a nice witchy boy like you end up trafficking with our sort?"

"I made a deal."

"You made...you made a deal? Like...you know, a deal with the Devil? A real one?" Kit asked, his eyes fixed disbelievingly on West's face. "Sold your soul and everything?"

"He didn't want my soul. He wanted a favor. It was stupid, alright? I was just a kid and I'm..." West sighed and gnawed at the skin around another finger. "I'm lucky it didn't turn out worse. I'm lucky he didn't want a real favor. I just, you know, I answer questions."

Kit stared at him and West felt himself growing warm under his gaze. "What kind of deal?"

His face flushed even hotter and he thought he must have been visibly red by now. "I don't want to talk about it."

Instead of teasing or pressing the matter, Kit nodded. "Alright." He pulled out his phone and looked at the time. "I have to go pick up Riley soon."

"No, you don't."

The demon raised an eyebrow. "Alright, fine, I've got a couple hours, but you know sometimes people are just lying to be polite."

"Yeah, I know, except it doesn't feel polite once you know everyone's lying."

"Okay, let's see if this one passes the test. I'm gonna go 'cause I don't know what else to say, I'm dying for a smoke, I want to wash all those clothes because I'm worried they've somehow been contaminated, and I need, like, half an hour to decompress."

"You need more than half an hour."

The demon gaped. "How...how could you *possibly* know if that's a lie or not?"

West shook his head and explained, "Oh, no, I don't. I'm just saying that I don't think half an hour's long enough."

Kit stood and fished his keys out of his pocket. "You'd be surprised, I've become amazingly efficient at getting all my emotional baggage crammed into my subconscious."

"I don't think that's the same as decompressing." West stood, too, putting his hands in his pockets so he wouldn't rip any more skin off his fingers.

"We can debate that some other time."

West shrugged.

"Maybe over dinner?" the demon asked without really looking at him.

Absolutely not. Hooking up would have been one thing, but all of this was straying dangerously towards the beginning of a relationship and *not* just something casual. Casual didn't involve any of the topics they'd covered today. Casual was pretending to care about what kind of music the other person liked or what they had thought of the most recent season of *Game of Thrones*.

West chewed the inside of his lip for a second, trying to think of a nice way to say no, but he answered instinctually before he'd had a chance to consider all the varied implications of getting dinner together. "Sure."

Even Kit looked surprised. "Really?"

Now was his chance to backpedal. "Yeah."

"I, uh..." The demon smiled, tentative at first, but then started to grin. "Cool. Yeah. I'll text you?"

West couldn't even pretend that he didn't want Kit to text him at this point. "Alright."

"Good," Kit said. He jangled his keys. "Great."

West couldn't help but smile, too.

"I should go."

"Yeah." West crossed the room and opened the door for him.

The other man headed out quickly and made it halfway down the front steps before he turned back and said, "Bye."

"Bye."

West watched him go and didn't close the front door until Kit had gotten into his car and backed down the driveway.

Once he'd gone, West let out a long breath, trying to dissipate some of the jitteriness that had settled over him.

LAUREL CAME home that evening with her arms full of groceries. She struggled through the door and announced, "I didn't bother to ask if you needed anything 'cause I know you don't eat."

She set everything down on the kitchen table and returned with another armful of bags. "Are you doing another goddamn reading for the rabbit?" she demanded as soon as she saw him on the carpet with Mipsy on his lap.

"Yes," he lied, suddenly not wanting her to know that he'd done one for himself. The spread hadn't shown him anything particularly surprising. The two of wands, the Star, then the six of swords reversed.

Their predictability reassured him.

He swept up the cards and returned Mipsy to her hutch, giving her a treat before he closed the door.

"How was work?" he asked his sister.

"The usual," she said. She set the rest of her bags down and set to unloading the groceries.

He helped, filling his arms with perishables and heading towards the refrigerator. As he rearranged the freezer to make room for her ice cream, Laurel called, "West!" her voice sharp and worried.

He shoved in the ice cream and turned towards her. "What?"

She held up the suncatcher, pinching the chain between her

thumb and forefinger like it was filthy. "What is this?"

"Oh."

"What is it?"

He saw the assumption and worry rushing across her face. "Nothing," he assured, "Just, uh, it's a work thing."

"What do you mean a work thing?" she demanded. "You don't have a job."

"I work, though," he protested. He closed the freezer and took the suncatcher. "It's, uh, it's not something to worry about, really. It's not what it looks like."

"It looks like dark magic."

She might have been right but he didn't need her breathing down his neck as he tried to figure out what this suncatcher, Mike, and the woman Luella had seen had to do with each other. Especially because he shouldn't have been getting involved in any of this.

It was too late for that; even if he hadn't been interested in Kit, there was a murderer loose and West was starting to doubt the cops were equipped to find her.

Not that he was the next best candidate, but he couldn't think of any other options at the moment.

"Laurel, come on, since when do I traffic with that kind of stuff? I just...someone asked me to look into it, okay? They couldn't figure out what it was so I just, I thought grandma's grimoire might have a few answers," he said, not entirely lying. More like mangling the truth.

The first thing he'd thought when he'd seen the suncatcher had been that he needed to get a hold of his grandmother's grimoire.

"Mom's not gonna let you anywhere near that thing," Laurel warned.

"I'm not ten anymore."

"That doesn't matter, it's still not the kind of magic anyone should go playing around with."

"I'm not gonna *play around* with it. I'm just gonna see if I can find anything out about this symbol and then give it back."

"You should give it back *now*."

He rolled his eyes and took out a clean dishtowel from the drawer. He wrapped it around the suncatcher, sprinkled in a pinch of salt, then pulled out a length of black yarn. He wrapped the suncatcher carefully and worked seven knots into the yarn as he bound the thing, reciting the spell under his breath.

As long as he hadn't accidentally brought home some kind of cursed object, the knots would keep the suncatcher inert and harmless, if the thing even had any purpose at all. It was entirely possible that he'd overreacted and stolen something from Mike's apartment for no reason at all.

He returned to unpacking the groceries after that, hoping he'd done enough to soothe her worries.

It seemed he had, because she asked, "You like sushi, right?"

"No."

"Oh."

Afraid to know the answer, he asked, "Why?"

" 'Cause there's a new sushi place in West Hartford and Leia was talking about it. I told her you'd probably want to go."

"I..."

"And I know you've been blowing her off," she accused.

"I've been...?" True, he hadn't reached out to her, but she hadn't reached out to him either. "Listen, it's...we just didn't hit it off."

"You were supposed to call her," his sister reminded.

"I mean, I guess but...she could have called me if she wanted. Or sent me a Facebook message or something. It's two thousand sixteen," he pointed out, "And I'm not exactly into gender roles."

She sighed and crossed her arms like she did when he was being stubborn about something. "West. Come on, you've got to—"

"I don't *have to* do anything, Laurel. Alright? I appreciate you trying to set me up or whatever, but you know, it's not like I asked you to."

Her brow furrowed and he knew he was close to offending her.

"And it's not about Danny or anything, so don't go there," he warned. He intentionally softened his voice and suggested, "Worry about you, okay? Take some time for yourself instead of worrying about me. You deserve it."

Maybe pushing her towards a little self-care would get her off his back.

She sighed.

"Come on, take a mental health day. Go get a nice brunch and see a movie or something. Do a spa day. I bet Mom would go with you," he urged.

"I don't know."

"Yes. You deserve it."

"Maybe."

He hoped so. She needed to unwind before she drove him crazy.

Later that night, he saw her texting back and forth with their mother. A quick peek over her shoulder told him they were planning a mother-daughter day for Thursday.

An idea crossed his mind.

His mother wouldn't be keen on handing over the grimoire and he wasn't exactly thrilled about the idea of asking to use it or explaining why he wanted it.

She kept the book locked up in the attic and if he knew she was going to be out, there was no harm in stopping over and borrowing it for a little while. He'd learned his lesson about using any spells out of it, but sometimes to figure things out, it helped to look in less than appealing places.

Advances in medical science hadn't been made by leaving dead bodies un-autopsied and someone must have gone through a lot of unpleasant experimenting before they figured out what combination of dead thing and waste product made the best fertilizer.

Around ten, his phone buzzed and he scrambled to find it before Laurel could see it. Not that she had had any idea who Kit was, but he didn't want to play twenty questions about who he was and how they'd met.

So does it make me seem overeager if I want to see you tomorrow?

West bit his tongue to keep his face straight as he typed his reply, too aware that Laurel was watching. *Yes plus im busy tmrw anyway. Maybe Friday would be good.*

For the next few days, he had agreed to dog-sit for Tammy Rogers while she and her bride-to-be went out of state for something that had to do with wedding planning. Normally, dog sitting didn't take up someone's entire day, but their terrier had just about the worst case of separation anxiety he'd ever seen and had the potential to literally tear their house to shreds if left unattended.

Friday it is then.

West reread what he had sent before and realized that it could be interpreted as curt. He tried to think of a way to do a bit of damage control and sent *good looking forward to it. Hows the rest of your day been?*

Oh you know, standard Monday stuff. Watched wild kratts til I thought my eyes would bleed, put the kid to bed and now I'm trying to get some work done.

West didn't know what to make of that and didn't know if he should text back if Kit was trying to get work done.

But the demon had been the one to text him in the first place; Kit sent a follow-up message asking West how his night was going.

He answered and tried to think rationally about what he was doing. He could already see about a dozen ways all of this could go south, including trying to tell his mother or sister that he was going on dates with a demon.

A demon whose worst flaw was no longer being a smoker, it was having an arrest record and a former drug habit.

Kit would never have gone over smoothly with either of them, not even if he'd worked for Greenpeace. He didn't even want to start thinking about what his friends would think of the guy.

He told himself not to worry about it. Plenty of things could change between now and Friday. Either of them could come to their senses, for example. And even if they followed through and got dinner, there was no reason to think this would end up being anything more. It had been at least half a year since he'd even been on a second date and West didn't think that this chain-smoking demon would be any different from the other crappy dates he'd had.

No, they'd get dinner and maybe they'd end up pawing at each other in the car. Maybe if it had been a really good dinner, they'd do more than cop a feel and West would get that hook up he'd been itching for.

Probably a blowjob on the side of the road or something like that. West didn't think he'd be invited back to Kit's place and had no plans to let the demon and his sister ever be in the same building.

That would be the end of it. Things would peter out. They always did after somebody had an orgasm. No one ever looked as good as they had after a few drinks and a long time without sex; West figured Kit had to be the same. All the aloof charm of his confidence would fade, replaced with the taste of cigarettes and an awkward car ride home.

That's all Kit was. An itch to scratch, a hook up that had been interrupted and gotten some kind of bizarre extension.

West needed to get him out of his system.

May 6
Thursday

IT SHOULD have felt more heinous to go behind his mother's back like this, but West's only worry was that she could come home early. She had picked up Laurel for their mental health day, brunch followed by a hike, to be ended with a DIY spa day at Laurel's.

West had to get the book and get home to hide it before they returned, but he had hours to spare. He'd taken Laurel's car without asking and didn't want to deal with the repercussions of that, either. He knew if he had asked, she would have said yes, but she also would have peppered him with a thousand questions about what he was doing and where he was going. In a town as small as theirs, it was hard to make up a lie about working for someone or visiting a friend when Laurel was just as likely to run into that person while she was out.

He slipped into his mother's house, greeted with the smell of fresh bread and cinnamon. She must have been on another one of her baking sprees. Once a month, his mother would spend a week making all kinds of baked goods, everything from sugar cookies to challah bread. It was also when she'd spend time knitting tiny sweaters for her cats; West assumed it had something to do with PMS and would take his mother's nesting over Laurel's headaches and bad moods any day.

As he walked upstairs, passing a thousand and one pictures of him and Laurel, he reconsidered, recalling what it was like to be the focus of his mother's domestic energy. His teenage years had involved spending a lot of time avoiding his mother and her calm, open way of dealing with puberty.

She had been supportive and encouraging, but there had been times when West had wanted a lock on his door more than he'd wanted to talk about how it was important to explore his own body before he tried to explore anyone else's.

In the attic, he had to sift through three different trunks before he found the grimoire buried all the way at the bottom of the one that had been shoved into the back of a crawl space. His grandmother might have been into some dicey magic, but West didn't think the book warranted that kind of treatment. It wasn't like the book could do anything on its own.

Spells could only be dangerous if someone was casting them. A mage had said that to him once, though the arcane magic that mages used tended to have more explosive results when poorly cast.

West flipped through the grimoire briefly, checking to make sure that it did have passages dedicated to the kinds of symbols like the one on the suncatcher.

Once he'd confirmed that it did, he placed it in his backpack and started putting things away. He took more care repacking things than he had unpacking them and stumbled across a shoebox full of old pictures.

After just a glance at a few of them, he was sucked in and spent fifteen minutes looking at his childhood captured on photo paper. Him and Laurel, always together, always opposites. She was pale and freckled, round-faced with chubby cheeks, her hair a blaze of golden curls, and him, a scrawny dark-haired and bronze-skinned boy trying to open his eyes as wide as possible so no one would tease him about having his eyes closed in every picture. It made him look sort of wild-eyed and untrustworthy. Luckily by high school, he'd given up on that.

His phone buzzed, taking him out of his recollections of a summer visit to a Rhode Island beach.

He checked it, dreading that it would be Laurel telling him they were heading home early; it was Kit, asking if he had allergies.

Just dogs he replied. He closed the last trunk but didn't put away the photographs. He stowed them under his arm and headed downstairs, thinking that Mother's Day was coming up soon and that doing something with these would be better than shelling out money he didn't have for a gift his mother probably wouldn't get much use out of.

When he'd gotten in the car, he received an answer from Kit. *Shit well there goes my plan to take you to a kennel.*

Over the past few days, Kit had sent him half a dozen questions out of the blue and usually in the middle of the night, about whether West liked this or if he'd ever had that.

Sorry to disappoint.

The next response came as West was driving and it took all his self-control not to text and drive, especially when he got a second message.

As soon as he'd parked in the driveway, he read the messages. *I'll come get you at six,* followed by *if that's okay with you?*

Come get him? West hadn't been expecting Kit to pick him up.

Laurel would definitely be home by six on Friday.

West pushed those thoughts away; she was his sister, not his guardian, and he didn't have to tell her that he was going on a date or let her know who he was going with.

He told Kit that six was fine and didn't hear anything back.

That was just as well. He took the suncatcher from where he'd stashed it on top of the fridge and brought it and the grimoire down into the basement. His pursuit of the symbol's meaning was delayed by a fifteen-minute search of the entire house to replace the lightbulb in the bedside lamp he never used.

When he finally had light to read by, he cracked open the grimoire and started on page one. His grandmother had recorded her spells and bits of knowledge haphazardly, in order by how she'd learned them, not by subject.

As he combed through the book, carefully reading over the handwritten passages, he thought about how normal his grandmother had looked, another scrawny old lady with short, fluffy, pink-tinted hair. She'd always matched her cardigans to her shirts; the only times he'd ever seen her without a cardigan had been on sweltering hot days when everyone else had been drenched in sweat.

But here was the same handwriting he'd seen on birthday cards telling him how he could curse someone for cheating on him, followed by another meant to ruin the looks of anyone he thought might be flirting with his partner.

He made it about a quarter of the way through the book, no longer looking to glean information about just the symbols, but strangely fascinated by the spells and insights his grandmother had penned. He didn't think he would ever have the desire to make someone's teeth fall out, but it was interesting to see how he could go about it if he decided he did.

When he heard movement upstairs, he stashed the book beneath his mattress and headed up, knowing they would be calling down to him sooner or later.

As soon as he appeared, Laurel said, "You drove my car."

"How could you possibly know that?" he demanded.

"Because you left the windows down."

He rubbed his face. "Yeah sorry. I had to run out and get something."

She raised an eyebrow and crossed her arms.

He gave a pointed glance towards their mother, who was bustling around in the kitchen, and said, "I'll tell you about it later."

"Oh." She looked towards their mother, her face drawn with concern. "Uh..."

" 'Cause Mother's Day," he whispered.

"Oh! Oh, alright," she said with a nod. "Come in the kitchen, we're doing face masks."

He followed her into the kitchen, not displeased at all with the chamomile and lavender mask that his mother smeared all over his face. He could have done without the New Age meditation music she'd put on, but he'd learned to mostly tune it out at this point.

"West, you're so tense," his mother told him as she spread the mask over his cheeks.

"I'm not."

"You are. You're keeping secrets."

"Mom."

"I can tell when you're not telling me something," she admonished. She stepped back and looked him over, then added a little more goo to his forehead.

"I'm not telling you a lot of things," he told her, "But that's not the same as keeping secrets."

"What kind of things aren't you telling me?"

"I don't know, Mom, do you want me to text you every time I use the bathroom?" he asked, hoping to dissuade her.

He should have known better because she only asked, "Why, are you having tummy trouble?"

He groaned. "I'm twenty-seven, not five so…"

"Well, are you?" his mother pressed.

"No."

She pursed her lips and shook her head at him, then went to do Laurel's mask. "If you are—"

"Mom, seriously, if I need help with something, you are the first person I will ask," he said. "I promise."

"I hope so."

"Besides, this is supposed to be relaxing, isn't it? Why don't you ask Laurel about what's got her stressed out?" he said, trying to redirect.

"Laurel and I did a lot of talking."

"Yeah, West," Laurel said. "You should try it sometime."

"I talk."

Together his mother and sister let out twin snorts of disbelief. He hated when they did that. Luckily, neither of them pushed the issue.

Once they all had their faces coated, the next step was some kind of coconut oil concoction for their hair, which his mother assured would make it shiny and not greasy. He conceded to that and by then, he'd surrendered himself to everything else, including a sugar scrub and manicure.

Dinnertime time found him sitting on the living room floor, freshly showered, scrubbed, and wearing his favorite pajamas, painting Laurel's toenails. Mipsy hopped around, sometimes stopping to sniff at their plates and steal a grape or a cherry tomato.

They'd abandoned the New Age music for reruns on HGTV.

He grabbed his phone and insisted on having the two of them crowd in closer so he could take another selfie. Laurel had called him 'such a Millennial' and he tried to pretend she meant it in an affectionate way. His mother had initially seemed irritated by his need to document the night, but by the sixth set of photos, she'd given in and started to pose just as much as he had, especially after he'd shown her all the likes and the handful of comments saying that his mom was hot.

Getting a few of these printed would be a perfect addition to the Mother's Day gift he had in mind if he remembered to do it in time.

Friday

WEST SPENT the morning having the new photos printed and gathering the supplies needed for making a scrapbook. Making an entire scrapbook with two days' notice was a daunting task and he didn't know if he'd manage to get everything done in time, but his mother hadn't ever been one for deadlines. He could give this to her in June and she'd still be bragging about it for months.

He easily passed the first part of the morning gluing in pictures and adding captions, but as the time grew closer to six, his thoughts drifted to other things.

Kit had texted him once, just to confirm, and then hadn't said anything for the rest of the day.

At five, West showered again and spent a quarter of an hour standing in front of his closet, recalling Kit's accusation of being a hipster.

Simple would be best, except that West had two types of clothes: garish or thrifted. Even the clothes he'd worn when he'd had an office job had that borrowed-from-my-grandpa/found-in-a-dumpster vibe. He didn't know when that had become his main aesthetic.

As the clock ticked closer to six, he abandoned the idea of finding the perfect outfit and settled on wearing anything that covered most of his body.

He climbed into a pair of overalls so old that one of the knees had worn out without any assistance and a tee-shirt that had an ugly floral print, but had only cost two dollars. He stared at himself in the mirror for a second, cuffed the overalls and shoved his feet into low-top purple Chucks. He limited himself to three rings, one necklace, and two bracelets. He hoped the outfit said 'casual.'

All he wanted was something casual.

That and Kit's tongue in his mouth again.

And to impress him.

He jogged upstairs before Kit could do something like ring the doorbell. As he made for the front door, Laurel called, "Westley!"

He froze. "What?"

"You have a date," she accused, her narrowed eyes sweeping over him.

"No."

"You absolutely do. Look at you."

He shrugged. Maybe he had spent a little more time on his hair than he usually did and maybe this outfit had not been so effortlessly thrown together as he'd pretended when he'd been pulling it on. Maybe he'd spent all day thinking about what to wear. "It's not a date."

"Bullshit."

He peered out the kitchen window and then at the clock. Five minutes.

"It's not a date," he told her again, as though saying it would make it true.

He glanced out the window again and saw Kit's black Subaru pull into the driveway. He bolted out the door, slamming it behind him, and skipping down the front steps. He climbed into the car so fast that Kit ogled him.

"Hi," West announced, his face hot.

"Hi. You in a hurry or something?"

West glanced towards the house and saw his sister's face in the kitchen window. "Sort of."

Kit looked towards the house, but didn't ask any questions, just put the car into reverse and headed down the street.

After a few minutes of quiet, Kit asked, "So that was, what a roommate?"

"Sister."

Kit nodded and didn't ask anything else about the topic. "I, uh."

West waited, but when he said nothing, he prompted, "What?"

"Nothing. Just. You look nice tonight."

West couldn't help wrinkling his nose, not sure why the compliment reminded him that Kit was so much older than he was. "Thanks."

"Oof, that face. Are compliments not trending right now?" Kit asked.

West snorted.

"Was I supposed to do it with a hashtag or something?" the demon asked.

West rolled his eyes, not sure what he was supposed to say to that. He could tell Kit was only teasing and got the sense that the other man might have even been nervous. He fished his phone out of his pocket and fiddled with it, flicking between apps but not actually looking at any of them.

"Where are we going, anyway?"

"It's...it's kind of like a two-part thing," Kit said.

"What, like dinner and a movie?"

"Kind of," Kit confirmed, but added after a moment, "As long as you don't have any qualms with eating outside. I kind of figured that you probably wouldn't, you know, being a witch and all. You're supposed to be, what, all in tune with nature?"

"Yeah, that's what they tell me."

"The weather's been really nice."

"Mmm." West looked out the window. The past few days had been gorgeous, the kind of spring weather that he'd given up on after such strange weather patterns for the last few years.

"I kind of thought we could grab something and bring it up to this, I don't know, you've probably been there, that little area in Danson Park that overlooks the river?"

"Yeah, I know the one you're talking about," West confirmed. He'd been there loads of times as a kid.

"Good, cool."

There was something about being in Kit's car that felt alien, though West couldn't put his finger on what it was. Maybe he was seeing all the tell-tale marks of fatherhood he had missed the first time, including a container of wet wipes and packages of fruit snacks crammed into the cup holders. Maybe it was nothing more than being in the car with a near stranger and not knowing what it was that Kit expected out of the night.

He ran the pad of his thumb over his nail, smoothed by the manicure his mother had given him; the sensation pulled at him, freeing up the part of his mind that had been worrying about this date.

He realized what it was that had put him on edge. Something was missing.

"You, uh."

Kit glanced his way. "What?"

"You don't smell like cigarettes today."

The demon gave him a half-smile. "I've been with Riley all day," he said as though it explained everything.

"Oh."

The smile on his face turned quizzical and a little disbelieving. "What? You don't think I smoke around my kid, do you?"

West shrugged. "I don't know." He tried to think of something else to say. "How's it been having the rabbit back?"

"Good. You think I'd brought him the Holy Grail, showing up with that thing. He's been sleeping like a baby."

"That's good."

"Yeah, better than trying to tell a sitter how to calm him down when he starts screaming about it," Kit admitted. "Not that I wouldn't be screaming if I was him. I mean, shit, his dad just died. It's just that, uh...you know, he...When he gets upset like that, he..." Kit trailed off. "Listen to me, you don't want to hear about this."

"No, it's fine."

He shook his head. "Never mind, really."

West left it alone.

It wasn't until after Kit had parked in front of a deli and they'd were walking back out with sandwiches, that Kit abruptly began, "Listen, I, uh...I don't want you to think that I'm telling horror stories or anything. It's just the way he is, alright?"

"What?"

"Riley. About...he's got a couple things that he needs to work on but he's *four*, what four-year-old is perfect? I'm not trying to sound like he's a problem."

"Oh, um...I didn't think you were," West assured.

" 'Cause a lot of people do. They say things like...like, 'oh you must have so much patience, I could never do it.' That it must be *so hard*. Shit like that." Kit raked his hand through his hair, messing it completely, but somehow making it look better than it had before. "It's not like that."

"Sure."

"But you know, I just...I feel like I've got to warn people before they meet him just 'cause he might, you know, he might do something weird. It's a shitty feeling, worrying that people are gonna have a conniption over your kid."

West rubbed his nose. He hadn't imagined that they'd be talking about any of this. He hadn't considered what they'd talk about, but the nuances of parenting hadn't been a topic that had crossed his mind. It definitely wasn't something he could contribute to. "Should I consider myself warned?"

Kit titled his head and sort of smiled. "No, that was me venting. I kind of...I don't know, I feel like I don't have to warn you."

"Don't give me too much credit," West told him, not sure that he even wanted the responsibility of meeting his son or for Kit to have the idea that West somehow would be totally relaxed about it.

Kit looked him over and said, "You really don't want to talk about my kid, do you?"

West shrugged, not sure how much of his unease had been displayed on his face. "I don't know anything about kids."

"Alright, fine, then you think of something to talk about," Kit challenged.

West tried, he really did, but he was unable to find any topics that stuck. He burned through the usual ones, not wanting to ask too much about his job or the rest of his family. Finally, he asked, "Did you grow up around here?"

"It took you that long to think of that?" the demon asked.

Kit had already driven them all the way to the park.

"Here I was thinking you were going to have something interesting to say."

West scowled and clambered out of the car. He didn't wait for Kit and headed off towards the walking trail he knew they'd have to take to get to the overlook Kit had mentioned.

He could hear the sound of Kit's boots crunching across the gravel parking lot. More than that, he could feel his eyes on him. He turned around, his mouth pulled into a scowl. "What?"

"You really do look cute."

He rolled his eyes.

"Oh, I'm sorry, I meant hashtag mancrush Monday."

"Holy shit, you're so old," West groaned and pressed on, hoping that getting on to the trail and among the trees would make him forget how much older Kit was.

"Forty."

West whirled to look at him. "You said you were thirty-nine."

"Yeah, there's these things called birthdays. They come around once a year and—"

"Shut up."

Kit grinned at him, but then the smile started to slip off his face. "It's not gonna be a problem, is it?"

His voice had a tinge of vulnerability to it and that made West wonder what it felt like to be a gay, single father at forty. It sounded like it would be hard to get a date, let alone get into any kind of relationship.

It sounded lonely, having to peel away at the layers of labels, presenting each one to a date and wondering if that would be the thing that made them start to second guess whether or not it was a mistake to go on a second date.

The demon cleared his throat and had his usual brashness back when he said, "I'm sure a hot young thing like you has lots of prospects—"

"Prospects? Seriously. Are you sure you're only forty?" West demanded, hoping it came across as teasing instead of mean.

"I'm just saying. I get it, I guess."

"Yeah, well, if I didn't want to be here..." West said and put his hands into his pockets.

Kit didn't ask him to spell anything out. He quickened his pace a little until he'd caught up to West. They walked together in relative quiet; Kit had been right about the weather, it was a gorgeous day.

He'd shucked off his leather jacket and left it in the car, leaving his arms exposed again. West couldn't keep his eyes from wandering over the tattoos, curious to know how many more he had and what they would be.

The ones he could see were free of any kind of common theme or art style.

"Laurel has this hummingbird tattoo," West began, catching Kit's attention, "And anytime someone asks her what it means or anything like that, she gets all out of sorts and says 'it means I like hummingbirds.' But I don't know anyone who just likes goat skulls."

"Now you do."

"Really?"

"What, is everything supposed to have a meaning?"

West shrugged. "I always figured people must have a good reason to get things inked permanently into their skin. More than just liking it."

"Not really," Kit said. "I like tattoos. I like getting them, I like having them. Not like, you know, I'm going about it all random but, you know, I don't have a monologue prepared on why I got any of them."

"Alright, well, you might as well just tell me about your kid some more 'cause I can't think of anything else to ask you about."

"Not interested in my taste in music?" Kit asked.

"No, I just know I've never heard of, uh, whatever spooky Mount Everest jazz band you were listening to."

Kit sucked in a breath and held up a finger, "Okay, so first of all, it was The Kilimanjaro Darkjazz Ensemble and second, that's not even what we were listening to on the ride over. We were listening to Nocturnal Emissions and they don't sound *anything* alike."

"Yeah, you're right, this one made me feel like I was surrounded by demons," West told him, "Like actual demons from a haunted house, like the ones that want you to kill your family."

"I don't know, most demons don't really dig the whole haunted house thing, the pipes are notoriously shoddy," Kit informed him.

West's mouth dropped open and he hurried to apologize, "Oh, I didn't, I didn't mean it like that. I really didn't."

Kit waved his hand dismissively. "No, I get it. You meant spirit demons. Different from corporeal monsters for sure. The nomenclature is a pretty contentious issue if we're being honest. One more thing we can thank the Middle Ages for."

"I'm sorry," West said again.

"Like I was saying, they both kind of fall into the dark ambient category but aside from that, they're really distinct sound profiles," Kit pressed on and went on to explain how the second band had gone about turning the sounds of babies sleeping into what had been the most actively unsettling thing West had ever heard.

"That's fucked up," West pronounced when he'd finished.

Kit shrugged, looking a little embarrassed like he thought he'd overshared. "What can I say? I've always been into that kind of stuff."

"Yeah, you're a real spooky guy, with your kid and your SUV."

The conversation had lasted them to the overlook. They spread out their lunch on the picnic table and ate in relative silence. West wolfed down his sandwich and realized he hadn't eaten much at all that day, too absorbed in his Mother's Day project and pretending he wasn't nervous. Kit ate with a little more reserve and West tried not to watch him eat.

"Your turn to talk," Kit told him.

"About what?"

Kit shrugged and took another bite of food, his gaze directed over the trees. The overlook provided a view of the small river and the surrounding flora, as well as the occasional squirrel, bird, or chipmunk.

Other people were out on the trail today, mostly joggers and people with their dogs. A few gaggles of teenagers. Not as many families, probably because it was dinner time.

"I saw a deer out here once," West said.

Kit glanced back at him, an eyebrow raised.

"It was super early in the morning. No one else was out. At first, I didn't realize what I was seeing but when I did it was kind of creepy actually. Not like I'm afraid of deer but I got that feeling you get when you're somewhere that's usually full of people but isn't at the moment."

Kit said, "Liminal spaces."

"What?"

"They're places where reality feels altered. Like, uh, twenty-four-hour gas stations at three a.m. or—" the demon elaborated.

"Or the middle of the night right after it's snowed. Before anyone has walked in it and everything is quiet," West murmured. "The little beaches next to ferry docks."

Kit grinned, his eyes fixed on West's face as he added, "Stairwells in parking garages."

"That's how you fall into the Otherworld."

The demon didn't laugh; his eyes opened wider and he asked, "What?"

"In places like that where things aren't settled right, you can fall right through."

"That's scarier than anything I could have thought to say." Something about the way he had his eyes on West's face felt intimate, like he wanted West to go on saying unsettling things.

West could feel his blood moving through his body, across his lips and through his chest. He didn't know if it was because of Kit's gaze or because of the topic they'd settled on. He had the sense now that things could crumble away if he thought about it too much.

Eventually, they stopped seeing more people and the sun started to sink lower and lower. Kit had finished eating by then and West knew that they weren't supposed to be on the trail after dark.

Luckily, he didn't have to be the one to point it out because Kit packed up the garbage and shoved it into one of the blue bins that dotted the trail.

"Ready to head back?"

West nodded and stood, but paused before he moved back onto the path. "You like all that kind of stuff, right? Scary things. Unsettling things."

"Live and breathe for it."

"Come here."

Kit moved a little closer, a half-smile playing across his lips. "Why?"

"Sometimes things are real and not real all at the same time," West warned, "This...it's not going to be real, but...it's the things that live underneath the real world. I can show you."

The demon didn't seem put off.

"Do you want to see?"

He nodded, the slightest movement of his head.

West rubbed his thumbs against his fingertips, then squeezed his hands into fists. He drew in a deep breath and rested one hand against the side of Kit's neck, his thumb settling in the hollow of his throat. He could feel the other man's pulse there, the same as he could feel his own heartbeat thudding in the pads of his fingers.

He closed his eyes and opened up the world's layers. He didn't do anything more than arrange Kit's energies to expose the layers and wouldn't have dared to touch them, not even for a thousand dollars. He didn't know if he had the power to manipulate anything here and he didn't want to find out what would happen if he tried.

There was no visible change in the world or in what he saw, only the overwhelming sensation that crept up his toes to his legs, over his stomach and chest, and settled over his face, making his skin tighten and his ears ring. Nothing had changed about the world because none of this was real, except that everything had changed. There were not just trees but the souls of trees, the essence of the ground beneath their feet, and all the vapors of the air between them.

"Listen," he whispered, hardly doing anything more than

moving his lips. "Don't move and listen to the trees. They're calling for you. You can't answer, don't try. Never try."

Kit swallowed, his throat bobbing beneath West's hands.

"Don't look behind you."

"What's behind me?" Kit asked, except West didn't think he'd said anything at all. He hadn't heard his voice, but he knew what he'd asked, all the same.

"Nothing. Can't you feel it? There's nothing behind you. All the nothing in the entire world is there. Waiting."

They stood like that, silent and frozen, listening to the muffled sounds of the world, the rippling of the water and shuddering of the leaves.

Everything rushed back when Kit moved in, touching his lips to West's and sending things back to how they should have been, unexposed and comfortably familiar.

It was the smallest kiss, softer than the trickle of raindrops down a window.

"Do you want to come look at my grandmother's grimoire with me?" West asked. "I think that symbol from the suncatcher might be in there somewhere."

"Yes."

Moonless night had swallowed up the world around them while they'd been standing like that. He fished out his phone and the light from the screen hurt his eyes, brazenly declaring that it was just after nine o'clock. Somehow, they'd been standing still for almost an hour.

Kit had his head craned back and his eyes on the sky.

"You don't have to get home to Riley?" West asked.

"He's with his grandparents for the night," Kit said, then lowered his gaze and elaborated, "It can be a bitch to find a babysitter who doesn't freak out when the kid smacks her."

West had no idea what he would do in that situation either.

He didn't have to think about it for long because Kit kissed him again, more firmly this time. Nothing at all like it had been behind the Knot, but a good, solid kiss that made his skin tingle. Made him press in closer, no matter that it was pitch black and they shouldn't have been out here at this time of night.

A branch cracked off to their left and somewhere else, something rustled through the trees.

"We should get out of here," Kit said, stepping back.

West took ahold of Kit's hand, not able to see more than a few inches in front of his nose; nor could he shake the feeling that something was behind him. He shouldn't have pulled that nonsense with showing him the layers. Dusk was a stupid time to be playing with things that he barely understood. He'd be lucky if something didn't follow him home after a stunt like that.

Kit stepped out onto the path, surefooted as West shuffled uncertainly behind him. West fumbled with his phone and turned on the flashlight, angling it so he could kind of see where his feet needed to be.

Kit glanced his way and, without pausing, gestured with one hand as though he were picking lint off someone's shirt. Pinched between his fingers appeared an orb of light, softer than the light of West's phone and illuminating a wider area.

"Huh," West breathed.

"Just a bit of devilry."

It didn't look at all like what demonic magic was supposed to look like. All the stories West had ever heard spoke of unpredictable power bent to the will of a creature that could come unhinged and turn that power loose on the world, or on whatever unlucky bystander happened to be closest.

This little bit of light seemed perfectly tame, not any different than the lights that a mage could conjure.

West turned off the light on his phone and wiggled his hand more securely into Kit's grip.

THE WALK back to the car in the dark took longer than it would have in the light; that and a stop at the gas station made it so that it was ten o'clock by the time West had Kit park his SUV across the street and down a little.

"We're in front of Hezzie's yard, she won't mind," West assured.

"And the reason I can't park in the driveway...?"

"Is the same reason you have to be dead fucking quiet when we go inside," West said.

He could see that all the lights in the house were off except for in his sister's bedroom upstairs. That meant she was either on the phone with someone or reading, or if he was lucky, it meant she'd fallen asleep with the book on her chest and the light still on.

Kit didn't argue and maintained his silence as they crept into the house. They made it through the kitchen and halfway to the basement before Laurel, her voice laden with sleep, called, "West?"

"Yeah?"

"Just making sure. How was your date?"

"It wasn't..." He glanced guiltily at Kit. "Fine. Go back to sleep."

"Make sure you lock the door."

"I did."

She called something else that he couldn't quite make out.

Once in the basement, West turned on the lights and Kit whispered, "Am I allowed to talk now?"

"Quietly."

But Kit didn't say anything. Instead, he surveyed the room, his eyes roaming over the futon and the bed, the dresser covered with various pieces of jewelry and the heaps of DVDs by the television.

West tried to ignore him as he pulled the grimoire out from under his bed. "I'm not supposed to have this," he admitted to the demon as he turned around, the book cradled in his arms. "My grandmother got into some heavy stuff and my mom...and my sister, they would freak if they thought I was—"

"Dabbling in the dark arts?" Kit guessed.

West nodded. "But I swear, I saw something that looked like the symbol on the suncatcher."

"Any idea what it might be?"

"Not really but I've kind of got this suspicion."

Kit said, "I love suspicions."

"Just...you said Mike *wasn't* into anything in the Community? I mean, other than you?" West asked.

"He got pretty far into me if we're being honest."

The casualness of the tone almost belayed the innuendo. West tried to ignore it. "I think it might be a demonic sigil."

"A what now?"

"Not the kind of demon you are, but like the kind of demon that lives in Hell," West told him.

Kit shook his head. "No, Mike wasn't into anything like that. He barely even believed that I was what I said I was and he definitely never wanted to talk about it."

West flipped through the book until the last set of sigils he'd come across; he turned it so Kit could also view the same spiky, angular sigils that filled the page. A half-dozen of them accompanied with passages about the entities to which they belonged.

"Skarn?" Kit read, one eyebrow arched. "Has the form of a snake, best summoned when eliminating vermin."

"Like I said, it's just a suspicion."

Kit closed the book and handed it back. "Like *I* said, Mike never would have gotten involved in anything like this. Maybe it was just, I don't know, a gag gift or something."

West set the book aside. "Not even if he was getting blackout drunk?" he asked gently, not able to comfortably voice the second part of the recollection. He hadn't been able to stop thinking about

Kit casually rattling that off at his ex-sister-in-law.

"Don't go looking into stuff too much," Kit advised, his tone sour, almost aggressive.

It wasn't the kind of aggressive meant to really be hurtful, though, just hurtful enough to end a discussion and make it clear that it wasn't a topic to be touched again.

Kit had every right to be sore about it, too; it wasn't exactly a first date kind of thing to bring up.

"You...you want to watch a movie or something?" West offered, not able to wrap his head around how lame he felt.

He'd have to look into the grimoire more on his own time. He shouldn't have been showing it to Kit anyway, he wasn't a witch and didn't have the right frame of reference for any of the spells.

It had mostly been an excuse to invite him back, anyway.

"Sure, if you want to waste time," Kit said. "Or we can cut to the chase."

There was that almost aggressive tone again. Something had struck a nerve and he wanted distance between West and himself. Maybe not physical distance, but definitely the emotional kind.

"You know, that's actually a term from the movies. Speaking of movies. Bad writers and directors used to pad the run time with all this extra stuff, you know, too much dialogue. Audiences would get bored waiting for the chase scene. Back in the silent movie days," West babbled. "So they'd edit it all down. You know. Cut to the chase."

Kit stared at him.

"So do you want to watch a movie?" West asked again.

"Not really," he admitted.

"What do you want to do?"

"I have no idea."

"Mmm, I don't know how true that is," West said. "You've got some kind of idea."

"Do you ever *not* do that? The thing with the lies?" Kit snapped.

"I wish I couldn't do it at all," West replied, "Every first date is eighty percent bullshit, you know? It *sucks* knowing that. And trying to make things work with anyone? Everyone lies. All the time. Most people are just lucky enough to believe each other. I mean, imagine knowing the exact moment when someone says 'I love you' and doesn't mean it anymore."

"That...I'm sorry."

"Whatever."

"No, I am, I'm sorry. I didn't know it was like that," Kit said.

"I know."

Kit hadn't been lying, but it didn't make West feel any better. It didn't get rid of the disappointed feeling worming over his skin.

He felt like the world had shrunk him down so he'd be easier to step on. "Listen, you don't have to stick around, this was stupid."

Without saying anything, Kit stepped in closer and hooked an arm around him, pulling him into an embrace. He added a second arm, pulling West in close and holding him tight. He only had about half a head on West; it put him at just the right height to kiss the top of West's head, which he did.

"It doesn't feel stupid, though," Kit said. "It feels like a good idea."

West huffed softly.

"Then again, I have pretty bad judgment..." he admitted.

Being close to him made West feel the right size again, comfortable in his skin, and not worried about what he should be saying or doing. He put his arms around Kit and leaned all the way into his embrace, able to hear the thudding of the other man's heart. Without the overwhelming odor of cigarettes, West could almost make out the smell under his cologne. He didn't think he'd ever be able to describe the scent exactly, but he knew it was the smell of Kit's skin. He knew it was something he wanted to get used to.

Without realizing it, West turned his face and brushed his lips against Kit's jaw. The scrape of stubble against his lips might as well have been sandpaper against a match.

Suddenly their mouths were together, warm and insistent.

Kit's hands found their way up his ribs and over his chest, unhooking the straps of his overalls to get to his skin. He pulled West's shirt over his head and drew him in for another kiss, cupping the back of his head with one hand while the other slid lower, down his back, but stopping there.

West stepped back, kicking off his shoes and stepping out of his overalls, stumbling a little in his haste.

Kit didn't notice, too busy peeling himself out of his own clothes.

At the sight of him, West paused, his eyes raking over the other man's skin, finding his chest and legs just as decorated as his arms. An owl here, over his ribs, and some kind of tree line encircling one ankle. A small, minimalist UFO and some stars over his heart, a lantern and a sperm whale on one of his thighs. They went on and on.

Here and there were spans of blank skin, some as wide as a finger, others wide enough for two hands.

West reached out to touch one of the blank spaces, over his stomach. The moment of exploration didn't last because Kit was kissing him again, drawing him in closer and pressing his thigh between West's legs.

West pressed back, aching.

He pulled Kit toward the bed, both of them shedding the last remains of their clothes and twining together. He almost didn't know what to do when Kit found his way beneath him instead of pushing on top of West. Kit kept him close the whole time. His mouth never strayed far West's and his thighs remained firmly locked around West's hips. Kit brought West inside of him and kept him there, drawing him deeper, rolling his hips to meet West's movement until they both teetered over the edge, panting and moaning.

Afterward, West buried his face in Kit's shoulder and didn't move. Moving would surely ruin whatever ill-advised impulse had brought them together and he didn't want to ruin anything. He wanted to stay like this, skin against skin, pretending that he could go on being just as unthinking for the rest of his life. He didn't want to worry about what Laurel would think if she found out who he'd let into the house without sparing a single thought for what he was.

He'd thought so little about it that he'd never stopped to get a condom.

He pulled back, the warmth of the moment shattered, and saw that Kit had a look on his face that said he might have realized the same thing, or at the very least had some sort of reservation about what they'd done.

"I, uh...I'm, um..." West fumbled for the right words, words that definitely should have passed his lips twenty minutes ago. "I'm clean."

Kit blinked and frowned. "What?"

"Like...you know, STDs and stuff."

"Oh my god, I didn't even think about that." Kit sat up a little bit. "I mean, shit, sorry, I am too, but I am *really* out of the loop on this whole dating thing."

West shook his head. He'd been doing a lot of stupid stuff lately, but this could have been the stupidest.

"I'm sorry, I should have said something, I kind of thought you knew," Kit said, sitting up more and running a reassuring hand over West's arm.

As much as he wanted to be soothed by that touch, to lean against him and not think about how stupid he'd been, West had to ask, "Knew?"

"Perks of being a demon include great night vision, cool magic tricks, and generally being pretty resistant to disease," Kit told him. "Which is lucky for me, 'cause I made some *horrible* choices in the nineties."

"Holy shit." Panic thrilled through West, his heartbeat doubling.

"No, but I am clean, like officially, I went to a real doctor and everything," Kit hurried to assure him. "God, don't look so scared. You're making me feel terrible."

West shook his head. "No, it's...it's fine."

Kit leaned in and pressed a kiss to his temple.

West melted against him. He didn't want to think about anything. He wanted to get back to that warm moment right after they'd come and things had momentarily felt right.

Kit wrapped his arms around him and nestled close, his skin warm and now smelling overwhelmingly of sex instead of cologne. Kit kissed him again and said, "I could watch a movie now if you wanted."

"I'll fall asleep," West warned.

"I'm fine with that."

Once they'd cleaned up and settled back into the bed, snuggled under the covers this time instead of writhing on top of them, they both fell asleep halfway through *Lawrence of Arabia*, which wasn't too shabby, considering that the movie was about four hours long.

West woke hours later in a panic, at first worried that he'd slept through his alarm and then not able to figure out why he was so warm. He checked his phone, wincing at the bright screen. Four a.m. Long before Laurel would be awake.

He shook Kit awake. "Hey."

"Mmm?"

"You gotta go."

Kit pushed himself up, his face blearily contorted as he asked, "I'm sorry, are you kicking me out?"

Immediately West felt like a scumbag and scrambled to explain, "No, not...not like that."

"Like what then?"

West tried to explain, his words coming out forced and shaky. "Listen, my sister's upstairs and she's, I mean, she'll freak out if she finds out."

"That you had sex?" Kit ventured uncertainly.

West hesitated to elaborate.

With a soft note of compassion in his voice, Kit asked, "You're not out?"

"It's...it's not that," West said, rushing to quash that assumption but skirting the truth.

Kit was able to guess anyway. "You don't want anyone to know you had sex with an ungodly monster like me."

"Hey."

Kit sat up all the way and threw back the covers.

West got out of bed and scooped up Kit's clothes before he could. "Kit."

"No, I get it, I'll go." Kit reached for his clothes and West felt more than awkward, he felt guilty.

West held out his clothes, but almost didn't; as long as he held them, Kit didn't have much of a choice about staying to hear him out. "Listen, it's not you. She'll freak out and, I mean, you don't need to hear any of that."

The demon practically snatched the clothes out of West's hands.

"No, I get it, trying to protect my feelings, right?" Kit sneered, yanking on his clothes like they were to blame.

"Kind of, yeah."

"It has nothing to do with being embarrassed." The statement came with hesitance and accusation, but also a tinge of hope. Kit wanted to be wrong about this.

West licked his lips, trying to think of the right thing to say. To think of what he really wanted to say. Easy lies came to mind, but Kit deserved better than that. He wasn't going to be something meaningless, some one-night-stand West had picked up in a bar or through an app.

"That's what I thought," Kit said when West took too long to answer.

"Hang on, wait." West reached out and put his hand on the other man's arm, worried he would storm out.

Kit waited, his face drawn tight.

"I'm not embarrassed," West swore. "But this is all, it's kind of a lot. I mean, we're living two really different kinds of lives. I, um, I want the chance to figure out what we're doing, where this is going, before I have to start defending it to my family. 'Cause I will have to. I don't want to worry about that yet."

"That's..." Kit let out a sigh. "That's reasonable."

West gave him a nervous smile.

Kit finished dressing, though with less aggression than he'd had before. He started to head towards the stairs before West had pulled on the rest of his clothes.

"Hang on, wait," West said as he struggled into a pair of sweatpants. "I'll walk you to your car."

They crept through the house together and out into the night. He followed Kit to his car and hesitated, not sure what he wanted to say or if he'd have the guts to say it.

He began, "You should..." but Kit glanced his way and West's words dried up. None of this had gone according to plan. He swallowed and licked his lips. "You should text me or something."

"Yeah?"

"Yeah. And, uh...we should hang out sometime. If you want."

Kit agreed, "Definitely."

West sucked in a shaky breath. "But for real, though, we should."

Kit snorted. "For real," he promised. He leaned in, his hand resting on West's waist and pulling him in. He kissed him gently, then stepped back.

"Bye," West whispered.

"See you."

West wrapped his arms around himself and stepped back, watching as Kit got into his car and headed down the street.

He still couldn't believe that he'd actually kicked someone out in the middle of the night instead of risking Laurel finding out that he'd slept with a creature. A shifter she might have tolerated and a vampire definitely would have drawn disdain if not outright disgust. A demon, though, well, she'd be upset about Kit just hanging around on the porch.

May 8
Sunday

After spending all of Saturday hiding in the basement under the guise of finishing his Mother's Day present, West finally had to face his sister. She had asked him about his date at least three times so far and each time he'd shrugged her off.

Now he was trapped in the car with her on the way to meet their mother for lunch.

"So how was your date?" Laurel asked as soon as she'd started driving and the doors had locked automatically.

"I told you it was fine."

"Fine doesn't tell me anything. You told me your date with Leia was fine and that was bullshit," she reminded.

He shrugged. "I don't know what you want me to say."

"Uh, like a name, maybe, would be good to start with. A gender. Literally any information."

He looked out the window. "He's just a guy."

"Alright, well, does he have a name?" she asked.

"Kit."

"What's he like?"

"He." He sighed and scrunched further down in his seat. "I don't know, he's just a guy." Even if he hadn't been skirting around the details, he didn't know how he'd describe Kit. He settled on a non-description. "He's nice."

"Cute?"

He shook his head right away. Cute wasn't the right word for Kit. Neither was handsome or good-looking or hot; none of those words captured the solidness of his presence or the draw of his easy confidence. There wasn't a word for the occasional flashes of worry or pain that would show on his face and make West's chest tighten. "He's, uh, yeah, he's attractive."

She grinned at him. "Attractive! How'd you meet him?"

He hadn't thought up a good lie for that yet. "I don't know."

"You don't know?" she asked, incredulous. "How can you not know?"

"It just kind of happened, I don't know, not everything has to be a meet-cute," he snapped.

"Shit, sorry for asking," she sulked.

He crossed his arms and hunched his shoulders.

She didn't ask him anything else. She barely talked to him for the rest of the ride and he had hoped that was the end of it.

As soon as he saw his mother, he knew that he had been wasting his time worrying about Laurel. He should have been a hundred times more worried about his mother. Laurel could work a spell and make a potion, but his mother had intuition, which made her dangerous.

She kissed his cheek and drew him into a hug; when she pulled back, she had a grin on her face. One touch and she had already gleaned more than Laurel ever would have been able to get out of him.

If she put her mind to it, she'd be able to untangle everything about the man whose aura was smudged all over West.

"You're gonna have to tell me all about it," she declared proudly.

He shook his head.

"Don't bother, Mom, West is keeping secrets," Laurel warned, pouty.

West shot her a dirty look. "It's not a secret, it's just none of your business."

His mother went to put a hand on his arm and he stepped out of her reach. He practically shoved his gift into her hands. "Come on, let's get a seat, I want to see you open that."

"Reservation's under my name," Laurel said.

He nodded and headed into the restaurant, his hands in his pockets. When they had been seated, he sat on the opposite side of the table from both of them. He kept his hands in his lap the entire time.

His mother narrowed her eyes at him.

She knew he was hiding something but he could manage that.

"Open your present," he urged, jutting his chin towards the bag she'd set on the seat beside her.

"Yeah, I'm dying to know what it is, he's been holed up in his room making it," Laurel chimed.

His mother pulled out the tissue paper, then extracted the scrapbook. At first, she frowned, confused, but when she opened the cover and saw the first page, her face lit up. She grinned, drawing out the crows' feet around her eyes.

"Oh, West, this is wonderful," she cooed. "Where did you find all these?"

He shrugged and changed the subject. "I had to call Auntie Merle and ask her about a couple of them. I couldn't remember for the life of me where that lake was."

His mother touched the photograph. "Bubble Pond. You were only a baby, look at those cheeks."

He nodded. In the picture, he had to be about two, which made Laurel around seven. She had him hauled up into her arms, both of them beaming at the camera.

She spent the rest of the meal going through each of the pictures, always having some little recollection to add. He almost felt bad that he'd used it as a way to avoid telling her about Kit.

"Oh, look at this, do you remember that? You thought those diamonds were the best thing you'd ever seen," she said, referring to the picture of him gazing longingly at the Hope Diamond. "You always were such a little magpie."

He twisted the ring around his index finger in response. "Wonder where I got it from," he said.

She laughed at that. His mother had never tried to moderate her love for sparkle or shine and today she wore a jeweled ring on each finger, along with about half a dozen glittering bangles on each wrist. The clinking of her bracelets had been a constant sound in his childhood, paired with every meal she'd cooked and bath she'd given him.

"Honey, I love this. Thank you."

He smiled at her. "You're welcome. I'm glad you like it."

His phone dinged and he rushed to put it on vibrate.

"Who is it?" Laurel asked, pretending to peer over the table.

"Just something for work."

His sister scowled immediately. "You dig up the worst people. I'm scared to even ask what you *do* with them."

"It's, uh, it's just consulting. The same thing I'd do for any witch," he said.

"Except they're *not* witches," Laurel pointed out.

His mother closed the scrapbook. "Honey..."

"Mom, it's not anything dangerous. Sometimes people have questions, I just help them get things sorted out," he insisted. "You know, just 'cause someone's a shifter or a vampire doesn't mean they're not allowed to need help with stuff."

Laurel crossed her arms and leaned back in her seat. "Well, I don't like them coming around my house. Especially not demons."

His mother audibly gasped. His mother, who had seen the filthiest part of the Counter Culture, who had at least six different people she was seeing scattered throughout the state, who had worked spells for dog fertility and made jewelry that evoked all sorts of genitalia, gasped at the thought of a demon coming to her daughter's house.

"Well, none of them have ever done anything bad to me," he defended lamely. He knew that this had to do more with the contract represented by the coins than any goodwill towards him on their part.

The coins guaranteed that they would get their questions answered and that West would go unscathed in return. Since the Devil was the one enforcing that guarantee, he didn't think anyone was too keen to breach the peace.

"Westley, that's...that's *incredibly* stupid of you," his mother admonished. "You have no idea what those sorts of people can do."

He sighed.

"Even if they're not *bad* people, West, they're still unstable. Even a vampire who thinks he's got his addiction managed still has an addiction," his mother warned.

"It's not a big deal," West insisted, wincing internally at her use of the word addiction. Vampires were addicted to blood in the way that humans were addicted to food. Calling it an addiction made some vampires try to go without, which lead to the kind of fevered binging that gave them a bad reputation.

"West, promise you won't—" she began.

"Mom." He rolled his eyes.

"Promise you won't get involved with those sorts of people."

"I promise," he lied without feeling an ounce of guilt. He couldn't control what kinds of people came to ask him questions and there was no backing out of a deal with the Devil. He'd resigned himself to that much years ago.

And he really did want to see where this was all going with Kit. No matter what his mother thought. Even if Kit's magic proved to be unstable, West didn't think he was capable of anything more dangerous than singeing something or putting on a light show.

As far as his taste in music and art went, plenty of regular humans had darker passions and remained perfectly harmless.

Some of them became serial killers, too, but West couldn't imagine Kit stalking the night to kidnap a victim and stuff him in the back of his SUV.

Serial killers didn't drive cars that smelled like applesauce, West was sure of it.

"West, I really mean it," his mother pressed.

"Mom, I promised, what more do you want? A blood oath?" he asked.

She sighed but didn't say anything else about it.

He ate a few bites of his food, asked Laurel how hers was, and then excused himself to the bathroom, making sure he had his phone.

He lingered outside the actual bathroom, checking his texts. Just the one message from Kit asking him what he was up to.

Out with my mom and sister.

A moment later, Kit replied *I'll go back to the dark pit I crawled out of in that case. Text me when you're free.*

West sighed and rubbed his face. This was going to catch up to him at some point. *I will,* he sent, then followed up with *for real.*

He returned to the table and made it through the rest of the meal without having to talk about his date or demons.

He spent the rest of the afternoon helping Hezzie finish up what she needed to prepare her garden and texting back and forth with Kit. The other man seemed to be gauging his interest in a handful of events.

The one that caught West's attention the most was Kit's plan to hike a local mountain with his sketchbook. It was also the one to which he hadn't been invited. That plan had been Kit's explanation as to why they couldn't catch a movie together on Thursday morning at the theater that did five-dollar matinees.

I like outdoorsy stuff, West sent, hoping he could weasel an invitation out of him.

I get kind of absorbed, I probably won't be a lot of fun.

I can manage to entertain myself, I'm 27 not 3, West told him, then thought that sounded too pushy so he quickly followed up with *not that u have to bring me im just saying witches tend to do well in the great outdoors. Don't feel obligated or anything.*

He thought he'd been too pushy because it took Kit a long time to message him back. When he finally did, the text read *I'm going early, right after I drop off riley. I think that conflicts with the time when I'm not allowed to come near your house.*

As long as u don't hold any black masses on the front lawn, I think itll be fine. West was not actually sure that it would be fine but the urge to make plans with Kit had become stronger than his urge to dance around his sister.

If you're sure.

Positive. Maybe Kit and Laurel would miss each other by some stroke of luck; maybe Laurel would see him but that didn't mean that she would be able to put all the pieces together. The time she'd identified Kit as a demon, he hadn't been in his car. It would be as easy as waiting on the porch and getting in before Kit could get out of his car.

Not that Kit would likely try to do that. He'd made it clear enough that he realized where he stood in the grand scheme of things.

Thursday

"WHAT ARE you doing?" Laurel asked.

West didn't look her way. What he was doing was obvious. He was waiting. He had been for about ten minutes, standing by the door with his backpack. He'd hidden his grandmother's grimoire in it, figuring that he could do some reading while Kit was occupied with his sketches. The demon had warned him several times that the hike would end up being more sitting than hiking.

At this point, even if West hadn't been getting butterflies at the thought of seeing Kit again, he would have wanted to go. Something had been making him restless lately, something no amount of gardening or yardwork for Hezzie or any of the other old folks in the neighborhood had been able to cure.

It was that his sister caught him smiling at his phone and he couldn't tell her why. It was that she asked what he was up to in the basement and he had to keep thinking of different lies.

"West?"

He glanced her way. "Mmm?"

"Where are you going?"

"For a hike."

"You didn't want to eat something first?" she asked.

"I ate," he said. It was true, he'd eaten, granted he'd eaten hours ago. He'd been up even earlier than usual, keyed up about not just seeing Kit but the idea that Laurel might figure out who he was.

"Ohh," she cooed. "Waiting on your date?"

"No."

She frowned.

Better to lie about that than have her glimpse Kit and put things together.

He returned his gaze to the window, then couldn't stand it any longer and went outside to wait on the porch.

It had been warm all month, warmer than it should have been in May, and the forecast predicted that the warmth would hold up. Even this early in the morning the air had a balminess and a touch of humidity.

Despite all that, he broke out in goosebumps when Kit pulled up in front of the house. Kit didn't even pull into the driveway and, as West practically bolted down the front steps to get to him, he tried to ignore the feeling in his gut that hiding Kit and making the demon feel like a pariah was not the right way to start a relationship.

There was that word again, creeping up on him anytime he dared to think about anything more than ten minutes in the future. Absolutely ridiculous, considering that their interactions so far had been little more than screwing on the first date, texting, and an attempt at playing junior detectives together.

That line of thought had West blurting, "Do people still think you killed your ex?" as soon as he got into the car.

Kit stared at him, his eyes wide; he regained his composure a moment later and started to drive. "I think the general consensus now is that I either had him killed or got him mixed up in something dangerous," he explained.

"But like, the cops are still involved?"

"Involved might be a strong word. Nosy, I'd say." He glanced towards West. "Why?"

"I don't know, that's how this all started, isn't it?" West asked.

"And you were, uh, incredibly disinterested," Kit reminded.

"So you're still looking into things?"

Sounding a little embarrassed, Kit admitted, "It's mostly been limited to combing through Facebook and seeing if Mike knew any short, sturdy brunettes."

"And did he?"

"Sure, but most of them are butch lesbians over forty," Kit said. "And most of them have short hair, which kind of rules out the whole ponytail thing."

"Oh." West shifted.

"And the more I think about it..."

"What?" West pressed.

"Uh. Well. Mike...he was into guns and all that. And he was in shape. Like...went to the gym twice a day, went to the shooting range every weekend," Kit elaborated. "So if this was just some regular woman, uh, at the risk of sounding sexist..."

"How was a five-foot-tall woman gonna get the jump on a beefy gun nut?" Kit supplied.

"He was literally beaten to death but he didn't get off a single round. His gun was still in his holster when..." He stopped talking, the words strangled more than they trailed off. He cleared his throat.

"We don't have to talk about it if you don't want."

Kit shrugged. "It's not a big deal," he said but didn't say anything else on the subject.

He stayed quiet for the rest of the ride, leaving West to stew in thoughts about murder and the unease produced by the current music Kit had on. It was a low, industrial kind of droning that raised the hair on his arms and made him feel like the car was about to shake apart into a thousand pieces.

When they got out of the car, Kit shouldered his backpack and stared down the hiking trail. He hadn't dressed for a hike, still in his ripped jeans and heavy boots.

Then again, neither had West. Old cut-off jean shorts and a t-shirt that had also seen the business end of a pair of scissors. He could feel the loose rocks through the thin soles of his Converse and wondered if he'd worried too much about the heat and not enough about the hike. He brushed those thoughts aside, remembering barefoot summers on his aunt's farm in New Avondale, ones where he and Laurel had climbed trees, smeared each other with mashed berries and pretended to be wood elves on the hunt for marauding goblins.

If he could survive that, he'd make it through a short hike.

He glanced around the parking lot and saw a man with three dogs stretching by his car, a dark-haired woman leaning against a tree, and a young mother vigorously pushing a stroller.

"Hey, Daisy Duke, you coming or what?" Kit called. He'd

already made it a few yards down the path.

West scowled and tugged down the hem of his shorts. He headed towards Kit and insisted, "They're not that short."

"No, you're right," Kit conceded. "Much more Kevin Bacon in *Friday the Thirteenth*."

West shook his head, not understanding the reference.

"Like, you know, with Jason Voorhees?" Kit said. "All those kids at Camp Crystal Lake?"

"No, I know, I just...I don't remember Kevin Bacon being in that movie." Of course, he likely hadn't really been paying attention during whatever Halloween party he'd seen it and couldn't be sure he was even remembering the right movie; as he recalled, there were about a dozen of them.

Kit shook his head. "Unbelievable."

"Sorry, slasher movies aren't my thing," West told him.

"No, just four-hour epics about—"

"Don't start badmouthing *Laurence of Arabia*," West warned.

"I wouldn't dare." Kit dipped his hand into his back pocket and came back with a pack of cigarettes.

"Don't."

Kit looked his way, one eyebrow raised. "Sorry?"

"I don't give a shit if you want to kill yourself with those, but you're not gonna go leaving cigarette butts lying around in the woods."

With half a smile, Kit put the cigarettes away. "Maybe they should put in more garbage cans."

"You didn't smoke at all last time we hung out," West pointed out.

"Yeah, well."

"Well, what?" West demanded, paying too much attention to Kit and not to where he was walking. A bit of loose rock slid under his foot and he wobbled dangerously.

"You alright?" Kit paused to look at him, one hand halfway towards West.

"Fine. Well, what?" West repeated.

Kit met his gaze for a moment, then headed off down the path, moving quicker than he had before.

West caught up with him, wondering if he should press the issue or not. He decided to leave it alone; the demon had put the cigarettes away and that should have been enough for West. He didn't need to know the reasons why Kit smoked under certain circumstances.

"You come here a lot?" West asked instead.

"Yeah, if I've got the time," Kit answered. "I haven't been able to get out here in a while, actually. All this stuff with Mike and trying to keep everything straight with Riley...I don't know why preschool starts so goddamn early. I mean, he's four, let the kid sleep in."

West caught a hint of untruth to that. "And what time does he go to bed?"

"Seven-thirty."

"And what time do you go to bed?"

Kit shrugged, then admitted, "Uh...it depends on the night."

"So maybe you should go to bed earlier."

"I work better at night," the demon said. "And besides, we do nap-rest-time at two anyway."

"Nap-rest-time?" West repeated.

"Yeah, I pick him up at one, we eat lunch, then it's nap-rest-time," Kit said as though it made perfect sense. "I told him he doesn't have to sleep, he can just lay there and rest. Sucker's out like a light in two minutes every time. Hey, come this way."

Kit put his hand on West's arm to get his attention, then ducked off the main path and onto a thin dirt trail.

West followed hesitantly, his eyes scanning the narrow trail for hazards.

"I'm not luring you to your death," the demon assured.

"Didn't think you were," he muttered. "Spider."

"What?"

"Stop walking, there's a big-ass spider right in front of you."

Kit stopped short, his eyes darting around until they settled on the large spider repelling down from the trees a few inches away from his face. He sidestepped the bug and said, "Good eyes."

The trail eventually widened to a small clearing littered with old fallen leaves and a few pieces of garbage, including a small pile of cigarette butts.

Kit beelined for the pile of butts, though, and crouched down beside them, slinging his backpack off his shoulder and fishing out a sketchbook.

West moved a little closer and saw that he'd settled himself in front of the aged remains of a large bird. It had been lying there for a while, at least since fall, West guessed based on how little was left of it.

"Tyto alba," Kit told him when he noticed West squinting at the pile of feathers and bones. "The common—"

"Barn owl," West finished.

"Ohh, good for you, you know your nomenclature."

"I'm a witch," he reminded.

A witch who didn't know proper names for plants and animals would have a hell of a time working a novel spell. A lot of them would have trouble naming their babies, too. Laurel had almost been named Latifolia, but her father had talked Diana out of it in time. West had just been lucky, though his mother liked to tell him that he'd come close to being named Phlox because he'd been conceived in Texas.

"Laurel and Phlox just didn't go together, though," she always said, "But imagine, Latifolia and Phlox, that would have been something."

At that point, Laurel, without fail, would chime in and say, "We're just lucky you didn't name us Cannabis and Erythroxylon," which always made West snort and his mother adamantly deny she had ever done coke.

A lie, of course, but no mother wanted her children to think she'd been a coke fiend in her younger years.

"Sorry there isn't anywhere to sit," Kit mumbled, his eyes fixed on the dead owl. He had planted himself on the ground not half a foot away and conjured up a light to illuminate the remains.

West took a seat on the leaves, skeeved by their feel against the backs of his thighs. He did his best to ignore it as he took the grimoire out of his backpack.

He'd gotten about halfway through and while he'd found a lot more sigils, he hadn't found the one he was looking for. He didn't know how many demons there were or whether or not his grandmother's list of them would be exhaustive.

Right now, he wasn't reading about demons, he was reading about how to make a nosy neighbor become violently ill whenever they tried to snoop or eavesdrop.

He briefly entertained the idea of casting it on Laurel; it would be easy to adjust it to make it so that she felt nauseated whenever she tried to unlock his phone. She didn't have any business going through his things like that and he wasn't sure if she was genuinely snooping or thought that whatever she found would be hilariously pathetic.

The next spell, however, made him reconsider ever taking

anything from his grandmother's grimoire. It was a curse to 'cause a miscarriage and he skipped right over it without bothering to even finish reading the ingredients. The next spell was much tamer, for making people go bald.

"Do you like to dance?" West asked when he came across a sigil for a demon that, when conjured and not bound correctly, would make the summoner dance in glass shoes until they bled to death.

Kit hummed a non-answer.

West looked up from the grimoire and looked at Kit, hunched over his sketch. He had an outline of the dead owl and was busy adding in details and shadowing.

About ten minutes later, as West compared a photo of the sigil from the suncatcher to one he'd found in the book, Kit said, "I can't dance."

"Can't or won't?" West asked, an attempt at being cute.

"Can't as in crowded clubs give me anxiety attacks sometimes, won't as in I feel like an asshole even trying."

"Oh."

Kit glanced up, his cheeks a little pink. "Sorry, that was kind of a heavy thing to drop. You can pretend I didn't say anything. Pretend I said some internalized homophobic bullshit about dancing being for pussies."

"Uh...anxiety attacks?"

"Like I said, pretend I didn't say anything." Kit closed his sketchbook and wrinkled his nose at the sight of West's phone. "You have service out here?"

"I have service everywhere." He jangled his phone so Kit could see the flag charm that dangled from the case.

Kit reached out to examine the charm, a small bit of enameled metal about the size of a postage stamp with pink, yellow, and blue stripes.

"Got it from this street vendor when I went to Pride last summer. She was selling, you know, the usual rainbow swag but I noticed her trying to help out this vampire that was like, puking his guts out with sun sickness...anyway, I went over to help and we got to talking," West concluded.

"You helped a vampire?" the demon asked with a lot of incredulity.

"He was really sick."

"I have to admit, I'm shocked that I'm not your first friendly foray into enemy territory," Kit said.

"I also made out with Delaney Kinspeak at junior prom and she was a werewolf," West said. "Is a werewolf," he corrected. "And we're not enemies."

"You kicked me out in the middle of the night."

West sighed and rubbed the back of his neck. "I feel pretty shitty about it if it makes you feel better."

"Weirdly enough, it doesn't."

"I know it's a shitty feeling—"

"Do you?" Kit snapped.

"Yeah, um, you might be a demon but you're not the possibly half-Asian lovechild of a mother who still says Oriental when she thinks you're not listening."

"I am not," Kit conceded.

"Anyway. Once...once I know what we're doing, I'll figure out a way to ease them into the idea." That was a lie; West knew there was absolutely no way to ease his family into the idea of him dating a demon. "Shit, I mean, do you even *want* to meet my family?"

Kit tousled his own hair and glanced off into the trees. "I...I mean. I don't know. I'd settle for *not* sneaking around, really. 'Cause keeping secrets feels like a bad start to...this."

West picked at his nails.

"Whatever this is," Kit mumbled.

"I was kind of wondering about that," West said, not looking up from his hands. He couldn't look up and he couldn't think of anything to say. His ability to form sentences had left him; his ability to even have coherent thoughts was nowhere to be seen, either.

Kit said, "I have no idea."

"Me neither."

"Maybe we can figure out what it isn't, though?" Kit proposed. "And not sit next to a dead animal while we do it."

West chuckled.

Kit stood and offered a hand to help West up; he didn't need assistance, but he took Kit's hand anyway.

As they headed back down the narrow trail back towards the main path, Kit said, "Not a one-night stand?"

"No."

"Or a hookup? I'm murky on the distinction between the two."

"Well, a one-night stand happens once. You can hook up with the same person again and still have it be casual," West reasoned.

"So are we just hooking up?"

"Something about 'early morning hike in the woods to look at desiccated animals' doesn't say hookup to me," West said, realized how snotty it sounded, and added, "We're not just hooking up."

"Spending time together?" Kit asked.

"Ugh! I hate when people say that. My mom says that all the time and I can never tell what the fuck she means."

"Dating?"

"Is this a date?" West asked.

"The way you said 'desiccated animals' made it feel like this definitely isn't a date," Kit pointed out.

"I don't know, you're a weirdo, maybe this is your idea of a date," West sulked.

Kit laughed and didn't seem put off at all by West's tone. "You're the one who wanted to come with me. I was trying to take you to get a drink or something. You know, one of those things that fits nicely into to the 'this is a date' category."

"People always go to get drinks. Every date Laurel ever set me up on is either dinner or drinks or something stupid like that."

"Alright, dinner and drinks are stupid, I'll keep that one in mind."

Heat swept over West's face and he scrambled to say, "No, not, not like that. You took me to dinner but it wasn't *dinner*. We didn't sit in some restaurant and stare at each other and try to make small talk about our jobs or where we went to school or stuff like that."

"And taking you out for a drink would be acceptable if...what, I brought you champagne on a yacht instead of buying you a beer?"

"First of all, I don't drink beer."

"And second?" the demon asked.

"I get seasick."

Kit laughed again. "You're gonna be hard to impress."

West shook his head. "I don't *want* to be impressed."

"Would you like to be disappointed? I've been told I'm a *huge* disappointment on a lot of occasions so—"

"No," West interrupted. "I just want, uh..."

"What?" Kit pressed.

"Ugh, it's super lame."

"Give it a shot."

West wrinkled his nose, let out a sigh and admitted, "I just want to hang out with you."

After a moment, Kit asked, "Isn't hanging out like hooking up?"

"Oh my god, you're so *old*," West groaned.

"Alright, forty is not that old!" Kit protested. "I've got at least eighty more years in me."

"Not if you keep smoking."

Kit didn't respond right away and when he did, it was only a mumbled, "So maybe I don't want to live to be a hundred and twenty."

West didn't know what to say to that and absolutely hated the squeezing sensation it had produced in his throat and chest. He moved in a little closer to Kit and touched his knuckles to the back of the demon's hand. Without a word, Kit turned his hand into to West's and wrapped their fingers together.

Their next stop along the trail didn't have any dead animals, just a bunch of ants swarming over an apple core that someone had left beside a bench. While Kit drew, West stared at a sigil in the grimoire as he munched on the celery sticks he'd brought and decided that it was definitely the same as the suncatcher.

Rithys. The name didn't ring any bells. The grimoire described her as a creature best summoned when something beloved needed to be fixed or healed.

He didn't know what to do with that information, but took a photo of it and marked the page. At home, he'd do a more extensive search on the internet. Someone out there who dealt in the darker arts would have more information. The trick would be finding an academic and not a fanatic.

He put the grimoire away, having had his fill of hexes and demons for the day.

Well. *Those* kinds of demons.

He took out a piece of celery and offered it wordlessly to Kit. The demon reached out and took it; he crunched into it then looked down at the celery as though it had betrayed him.

"What?" West asked.

"Nothing, no, I just..."

"What?"

"I thought it was a pickle."

"Why would I bring a bag of pickles with me?" West asked.

"I don't know, why would you bring a bag of celery with you?" Kit demanded.

" 'Cause it's a snack."

"Celery isn't a snack," the demon snapped. "It's crunchy air that people with eating disorders use as a way to pretend they're eating."

West's mirth dried up. He crunched into a stalk and chewed, not knowing what he could possibly say to that.

Kit seemed to know he'd misspoken. "Listen, I didn't mean people with real eating disorders just, you know, the gym bunnies and juice-cleansers."

West shrugged.

"West, I, listen, I can be a real asshole sometimes, alright? I didn't mean to hurt your feelings—"

"I *don't* have an eating disorder," West told him.

It was true. He might have passed out a few times at work, but he'd never gotten any kind of treatment or diagnosis. He'd never been sick, never been nothing but skin and bones like people with eating disorders were supposed to be. He just had a weight he liked to be at. That wasn't an eating disorder.

Kit closed his sketchbook with a sigh. He set it aside on the bench and scooted a little closer to West. "I'm sorry."

"Whatever."

Getting dumped had done a number on him, he could admit that. Losing weight, looking good had started as a good way to get back at Danny. It had only made him feel like he'd been fat and complacent the whole time, like if he'd taken better care of himself then Danny wouldn't have had eyes for other people.

Kit put the sketchbook away and shoved the rest of the celery he'd taken into his mouth. "Come on," he garbled around the stalk as he crunched. "Let's walk, it's too nice just to sit."

West got to his feet slowly and Kit snagged his hand. "I feel like all we ever do is talk about depressing shit. You have any pets? No dogs, right? What about a cat?"

"Laurel has a rabbit."

"Holy shit, tell me everything," Kit said with too much enthusiasm to possibly be serious.

"Uh, she poops a lot."

"That's about the worst description of a pet ever, they all poop a lot," Kit scolded. "What's her name?"

"Mipsy."

"Adorable."

KIT CONTINUED to ask him questions about mundane things, letting go of his hand at some point and putting an arm around his shoulder. West found himself perfectly content to lean into this one-armed embrace as they walked. They covered all the usual topics, the ones that West usually dreaded talking about, but also ended up delving into the finer points of when it was acceptable to stop a conversation to take a picture of a something.

That only came up because West had taken out his phone and snapped a picture of a blue jay in the middle of Kit's explanation of what exactly art rock was. He'd wanted to text it to his mom, not because she liked them but because she had an ongoing rivalry with a blue jay that lived in her yard.

"You're just jealous," West accused.

"How do you figure that?"

"You're the one making a big deal about it," West reminded. "All I did was take a picture, so you're either jealous that I took time out of your lecture or you're jealous that I wanted to take a picture of that bird and not you."

"That's dumb."

"No, it's not." West took out his phone again and pulled up the camera. He put it into selfie-mode and angled Kit so the light wouldn't wash out the picture. "Come on, don't make that face."

"What are you doing?"

"Over-documenting my twenties." He held up his phone, pressed his cheek close to Kit's, and took the picture.

"No, come on, don't..."

"Try smiling in this one," West advised.

It took a few more attempts before Kit actually smiled in any of them, but he did warm up and West showed him the best one. "See, you don't look like such a grumpy old grandpa in this one."

"I'm not grumpy," Kit huffed as he peered at the picture. "Send me that one."

With a laugh, West teased, "Oh, what, I thought I was addicted to this thing."

"Shut up, send it to me."

West shrugged and gave him a haughty look. "What if I don't?"

Kit slipped an arm around West's waist and pulled him in closer, closing the small gap between their bodies. He caught West's mouth with his, at first only kissing firmly, but then opening his mouth and sliding his tongue out to meet West's.

With his mouth close to West's ear, Kit rasped, "That right there, the being a brat thing you just did? You should probably be aware that I *really* like it."

West would definitely keep that in mind. He moved in for another kiss; just one, best not to get into anything indecent when there were other people out hiking today.

Kit pulled him back when he stepped away, though, and nuzzled his throat, then nipped his earlobe. He stopped when his phone dinged. He pulled back to check it, then frowned. "When did you even send this?"

West shrugged. "I'm a Millennial, I don't need to look at my phone to use it."

"Ooooh, shit," Kit hissed after he'd looked at his phone for a moment longer. "We gotta go."

"Hmm?"

"I gotta go pick up Riley. Fuck, I'm gonna be late."

They hastened back down the hiking trail, Kit's arm no longer around West, not even holding hands anymore. West hadn't realized that it had gotten late.

After a few minutes, West looked at his phone and said, "It's only noon."

"Yeah but by the time we make it down and it's like half an hour away from here, but your house is the opposite direction."

"Well, okay, but you don't have to drop me off first. If it's gonna make you late. I don't have anywhere else to be," West offered.

"Ummmm."

"I mean, I don't mind," he insisted, not sure why Kit would hesitate.

The other man threw a guilty look his way.

West stopped walking. "You don't want me to meet your kid."

"You don't want me to meet your sister and her brain is probably a lot more developed than a preschooler's," Kit returned with half a glance back. "Come on, let's go."

West resumed walking. "Well, if you decided that I'm allowed to be in the car with him, I promise I won't tell him that his dad puts out on a first date."

He didn't particularly want to meet Kit's son, but knowing that Kit didn't want to introduce them stung. He brooded. Kit must have been brooding too because neither of them spoke until they got to the car.

Kit fished out his keys, looked over West, and pronounced, "Well, you might as well lay eyes on him so you can decide if you don't want to date me anymore."

"He's a child, right? He's not the creature from the Black Lagoon or anything," West ventured, unable to understand why the topic had brought out so much bitterness in Kit's tone.

Kit huffed and said, "Yeah, you'd think that, but apparently it's a huge turn off for every guy I've tried to date for the last two years."

"Couldn't be every guy," West said as he got in the car.

"You're right, one of them was into fisting, which he told me, like, before our food even came the very first time we met," Kit conceded as he began to drive, "Which is what happens when you let your straight friends try to set you up on a date with literally any gay they can find."

"So hang on, what happened?" West asked, morbidly curious. "What's the rest of this story, like he was talking about him receiving or...?"

"Nope."

West grinned and had to ask, "To which you replied?"

"Well, first of all, he had hands the size of fucking...*cinderblocks*. I told him, you know, thanks but no thanks, to which he replied, now get this, hang on, that it was non-negotiable if we were gonna see each other."

West cackled, trying to smother it with one hand. "I'm sorry,

I'm sorry, what did you do?"

"I fucking left!" Kit declared.

"Like got up and walked out?"

"Yes, I got the fuck up out of my chair and walked the hell out, I do not need that in my life."

West snorted again. "Good to know, though, kinks include brats and do not include fisting. Noted."

"Brats aren't a kink," Kit protested.

"Google it sometime," West suggested.

Kit gave him a wary look.

"Oh, what, Mister Dick-eating-porn-zombies hasn't ever googled kinks?" West asked, one eyebrow raised.

"I was married for ten years."

"And?" West asked. He didn't know much about marriage. His mother had never been married and her sister was a spinster bordering on hermit. His grandparents had been married, but they'd been more like two bodies that existed in the same home than a couple.

"And Mike wasn't into stuff like that."

"Everyone's got a kink," West said, thinking there had to be more to it than that. Kit wasn't lying, though; he didn't have to be. Mike could have been the one who'd been lying to Kit. Second-hand lies didn't put up any red flags for West. "Found yours, that was easy."

Kit challenged, "What's yours, then?"

"My kink is not having this conversation on the way to a preschool," West said pointedly.

It had been one thing to broach the topic casually, but right now getting into the nitty-gritty of what he liked in bed felt like a one-way street to getting hard and having to talk himself down before they picked up his kid.

Kit snorted.

"Don't kinkshame me."

The demon rolled his eyes.

"So, like, anyway, you've got the rest of your afternoon booked, obviously," West began after five minutes of quiet where he dwelled on how much he would have liked to spend the rest of the day with Kit.

"Yeah."

"What about, like, tomorrow? Or this weekend?"

"Tomorrow?"

West shrugged. "Or this weekend."

"Tomorrow I'm going grocery shopping."

"All morning?"

"And doing laundry," Kit said. "Fridays are for chores."

West hummed a non-answer and looked out the window.

"But I'll, um, I'll text you about this weekend, though," Kit offered.

"Sure."

Minutes ticked by, neither of them really saying anything. Occasionally, Kit would offer an interesting fact about the music that played, like "This album is actually all one song."

Kit turned down a street and a sign announced the squat brick building as VILLAGE STREET AUTISM PROGRAM.

Off to one side and fenced in was a mulch-covered playscape that was absolutely swarming with children.

"I'll be right back," Kit said when he parked. "Hopefully."

He unbuckled his seatbelt and hurried into the school, almost jogging up to the front door. They had arrived about ten minutes after one, but West felt a little less guilty when someone else pulled up beside them and made her way inside, too.

West waited patiently for a few minutes. The sun shone directly on the car, heating the inside and making it stuffy. He got out and stretched. He'd spent most of the ride self-consciously hunched up, dwelling on what he was going to do about any of this. The more he thought about meeting Riley, the sweatier he got; he tried to blame it on the weather, but that was just lying to himself.

He wiped his palms on his shorts and retied his shoes.

He'd dated guys who were still in the closet, girls who had wanted him to 'tone it down' around their friends. He'd even hooked up with a Mormon who'd been on a proselytizing mission and had to talk him out of huffing exhaust fumes afterward. He could handle a four-year-old. He could handle introducing Kit to his family.

Not now, he reminded himself. Not anytime soon.

But someday. Maybe. If this thing was more than just an itch to scratch.

He straightened up when he heard Kit's voice, softer than it usually was, as he spoke to the flush-faced child clinging to his hand. "Bud, I know you don't like her—"

"I hate her!"

"Okay, that's fine, you can feel that way, but you can't hit people."

"She's *mean*."

"Hitting people is mean," Kit pointed out.

The little boy squealed and yanked on his father's arm. He wound up like he was going to smack Kit.

Kit let go of the boy's hand and stepped away from him. "Riley."

The child insisted, "It was *my* turn, it wasn't *fair*. It was *my* turn."

"It's all done now, we're not gonna talk about it anymore."

"I—"

Firmly, Kit told him, "No, if it's about the swing, I don't want to hear it."

Riley crossed his arms and stomped one foot.

"Do your breaths," the demon urged gently.

The boy huffed.

Kit crouched down beside him and poked his son in the belly. "Come on, show me those belly breaths. Come on, do it with me."

West watched as Kit pulled in a long breath and let it out slowly. Eventually, he had the little boy doing the same thing.

"Alright, how about a bear hug, show me that," Kit prompted.

Riley wrapped his arms around himself and screwed up his face, squeezing himself hard.

Kit ruffled the boy's tawny mess of hair, then scooped him up in one arm, pulling him in tight. "Isn't that better?"

The boy wrapped his arms around Kit's neck and the demon carried him the rest of the way to the car.

West looked at his shoes at they drew closer, feeling bad that he'd been staring openly at the two of them. He picked at his nails, yanking at a hangnail and making it bleed.

"I pick a song," Riley said when Kit set him down.

Kit handed over his phone and the boy scrambled into the car, buckling himself in and scrolling through the music on Kit's phone.

West sucked the blood off his finger and got back into the car once Kit had.

The boy handed the phone back to his father, stretching as far forward as he could.

Once the car started, a Gotye song that had charted a few years ago began to play and West commented, "Kid's got taste, at least."

Kit gave him a bit of a smile and put his phone in the cupholder. He turned around and said, "Uh, Rye?"

The boy, who had been patting his hands on his thighs, stopped and asked, "What?"

"This is West," Kit said with a gesture towards West.

The little boy squinted at West, then asked, "What your name is?"

"West."

Riley shook his head and waved a hand at West, not in greeting but in negation. "No, that's not a name. Try again."

Kit bit back a laugh. "It's a name, bud."

"No way," the boy declared. "West is like, northsoutheastwest. That's west."

"It's a nickname," West told him, not sure if it would help or not.

"What's a nickname for?" Riley asked.

"It's, you know, it's the short version of your whole name," West said.

"He meant what's it short for," Kit told him.

"Oh. West is short for Westley."

Riley nodded and went back to tapping his hands on his legs.

A few minutes passed, the song changed, and Kit asked, "What'd you do at school today?"

"Storytime about the Rainbow Fish and doing counting numbers."

"The story was about counting?"

"No." Riley went quiet, his eyes fixed on his hands. "Math time we did counting to ten."

"Rye, you can count to ten," Kit said.

"One two three four five six seven eight nine ten," the boy recited.

"You just counted?" asked Kit, sounding a little worried and looking at Riley through the rearview mirror.

"No, you...roll the dice, get the bears."

"Oh, alright," Kit said. "That's good practice."

"Tam didn't like to play counting," Riley informed his father. "He bit Miss Krista."

"That's not good. Did he say sorry?"

"No," Riley said. "I say sorry tomorrow for hitting her?"

Under his breath, Kit mumbled, "Ten minutes ago you hated her."

"Tomorrow I use kind words," Riley promised.

"Tomorrow you'll do your best," Kit told him.

West rolled down his window, wondering if he could open the door and roll out on to the highway without causing too much of a scene. He didn't belong in this car; he didn't deserve to be anywhere near Kit if he was going to treat him the way he had.

He listened to the pair of them chat back and forth for the rest of the ride, not knowing if he should chime in or when it would be appropriate to apologize for being a total asshole. The gravity of his misconduct hadn't sunk in until he'd watched Kit kneel on the sidewalk and take deep breaths with his son.

"You doing okay over there?" Kit asked.

It took West a second to realize that Kit had been addressing him and not Riley. "Uh. Yeah. Just thinking."

"Yeah, about what? Human rights violations?" he asked.

West shook his head.

When they turned down West's street, Kit asked, "Am I allowed to turn down the driveway or did you want me to drop you off down the block?"

At first, West didn't realize he was teasing and could only stare, wallowing in his own dumbshit-fuckery. Kicking someone out in the middle of the night and over what? Over Laurel and her stupid opinions. The moment passed when he realized Kit had been joking.

Kit parked in the driveway and said, "I'll text you about this weekend."

West nodded and got out, rushing out of the car, and closing the door harder than he meant to. He made it all the way to the porch before he had to double back to fetch his backpack. Kit had his window rolled down and handed it to him through the window.

"Sorry. Thanks," West said, his face hot.

"Yeah, didn't want you forgetting your book of curses."

West gave a nervous smile, clutched his backpack close, then jogged back up the steps.

May 16
Monday

AFTER WEST had gotten home on Thursday, he'd done a cursory internet search about the demon whose sigil had matched the suncatcher. As he'd expected, he'd found nothing. He'd put out the call to the darker areas of the Community, trying to stay vague and make it seem like he was nothing more than a witch with a passing, academic curiosity in the less practiced side of the craft.

Too much nosing around could get him embroiled with people who did more than dabble in dark magic.

So far, he hadn't gotten any information that he hadn't already known and by Sunday evening, it had gotten pushed into the back of his mind.

Mostly because he'd gone out for dinner with Kit. "Just something quick, Riley's with his grandparents for a few hours," Kit had said.

It had been quick, nothing but dinner at a local joint. It hadn't quite gotten his itch to spend time with the demon out of his system, but it was better than sitting at home and staring at his phone, wondering if Kit would text him or if West would be interrupting something by texting him first.

It wasn't that Kit didn't text, it was that he had better things to do than text all the time. He didn't always text back right away and usually, his excuse was entirely valid, either having been doing something with his son or being caught up in something with his work. So far, he hadn't lied about what he'd been doing either, which was a better record than West could boast.

For example, right now, West wasn't texting Kit back because he'd let Mipsy out of her hutch and had forgotten to close the bathroom door. He was in the process of luring the rabbit back out from behind the washing machine. He didn't plan to tell anyone that he'd been dumb enough to get into this situation.

He'd heard the notification, but Mipsy had wedged herself under the exhaust pipe. It seemed like a bad place for a rabbit and put a damper on his plans to do laundry. Laurel had warned him that scaring a rabbit could give it a heart attack and kill it. Throwing a load of laundry into their thudding, screaming artifact of a washing machine felt like a good way to do that.

"Mipsy, come on, Princess Bunny, let's go," West crooned to her, holding out a yogurt treat towards her.

Her nose twitched but she came no closer.

He clucked and cooed for about three more minutes.

The front door opened and he barely registered it.

Laurel's shadow darkened the bathroom as she leaned against the doorframe. "Did you lose my rabbit again?"

"She's not lost she's just...back there."

"Leave her, she'll come out when she's hungry," Laurel advised. "Kit wants to know if you're still on for tomorrow morning. Is that the same guy you saw on Sunday?"

He took his eyes from the rabbit and saw that she held his phone. He leaped up and snatched it out of her hand, more forcefully than necessary. "Fuck *off*, Laurel!"

She scowled at him, more frightened than angry. The set of her lips wasn't firm enough and her eyes had widened instead of narrowed. "What's your problem?"

"That you're always going through my shit, that's my problem," he snapped. He didn't feel as bad as he should have for scaring her.

"You're hiding something," she accused.

He ignored her and returned to trying to lure out the rabbit, his face hot, the blood in his ears pounding.

"Mom thinks so, too."

West scooted in closer, stretching his arm as far as it could go, and the rabbit took a small step forward, her nose twitching towards the treat. He continued to ignore his sister as she loomed over him, arms crossed. He cooed to the rabbit and drew the treat back.

She followed. A few more inches and he'd be able to grab her.

"West."

"I don't want to talk about it," he murmured, not wanting to scare the rabbit.

"I do."

"It's none of your business."

"You're living in *my house*," she reminded.

Mipsy took the treat from his fingers and West snatched her, dragging her in close as she tried to wriggle out of his grip. Clutching the rabbit to his chest, he pushed past his sister to deposit the rodent in her hutch.

"*West.*"

"I pay rent," he said, a lame defense, but a truthful one. He didn't pay much in rent but he paid it all the same; he tried to help out with the housework, too, to make up for the times in the past when he'd come up short and she'd let it slide.

"It's not about money, West, it's about you lying to me," she insisted, standing squarely in front of him.

"I'm not..." He sighed. "I just don't want to have this conversation."

"Why not?" she asked.

"Because it's gonna get ugly, Laurel, I know it is and I don't...I don't want to have to fight with you," he told her. "I really don't."

"I'm just asking you to be *honest*," she insisted.

He sighed again, more of a groan. He checked his phone, confirmed with Kit that they were still on for tomorrow, and made himself say, "Fine, but I don't want to hear about it. Not a single word."

She crossed her arms, an eyebrow raised as she waited.

He fidgeted. This had to come out sooner or later, especially if he was going to keep seeing Kit.

And he did plan on continuing to see the demon. Lots of him, if he had his way about it.

"You're really not gonna like it," he warned.

She didn't say anything, just continued to stare him down.

West had never had to come out to his family, at least, not in the sense that most people did. He'd had to do some explaining when he'd told them he *wasn't* gay, but that was about it. Everyone, from his sister to his grandfather, had pegged him as gay from first grade on, so they'd all been surprised when he'd taken a girl to junior prom.

His mother had even pulled him aside the day before prom, trying to tell him that he didn't need to hide who he was. He'd had to awkwardly explain to her that no, he was willing to get it on with just about anyone, not just boys.

He imagined this breathless, sick feeling was what it felt like to come out. He forced himself to draw in a breath and, his eyes on his feet, said, "It's just that the guy I'm seeing, he's...not...exactly human."

"Oh, come on, West, I'm not a bigot," she scoffed. "It's that half-fairy who works at the Knot, isn't it? You've been acting weird ever since—"

"He's a demon."

She said nothing.

He risked a glance up.

She had gone stock-still and a worrying shade of pink.

When a full thirty seconds passed in absolute silence, he bolted for the basement, locking the door behind him. He'd told her and she could do whatever she wanted with the information. It wasn't going to change anything, especially not the way he felt about Kit.

Especially since he wasn't sure how he felt about Kit, other than somewhere firmly in the dual realms of wanting to keep spending time with him and wanting to sleep with him again.

In an effort to distract himself from the dozens of dizzying scenarios playing out in his head, he turned on his ancient beast of a laptop, a relic from his college years. He stayed away from the social media pages he usually haunted and headed for the handful of message boards where he'd put out feelers about Rithys.

Some of the boards were open to anyone, but one of them was password protected and West needed to hit up an old friend from college to get the password.

Evie hadn't been an avid practitioner of dark magic when they'd first met at an Imbolc celebration, but that had been freshman year. Her craft had slowly gotten darker as the years had gone on, but West had kept in touch with her. Not only was she also queer, but she'd also been the only other witch on campus and sometimes spells needed more than one person. She'd always been a willing second for him, despite the fact that he'd shied away from any magical favor she'd asked of him.

She also willingly handed over the password when he requested it. It was a weird feeling to have someone send the password to a hidden occult chat board through a Facebook message. He felt like he should have needed to sacrifice a chicken or something to get it.

His mother had always warned him that people who practiced dark magic were too willing to share it, looking to pull in anyone who they thought would succumb.

West thought that Evie was just being friendly, especially because she sent a smiley face and asked him how he was doing, too. He told her what he'd been up to and shared that he still practiced the craft; he briefly mentioned doing readings at Beltane. She said that she was working in an occult museum in DC and married to a guy who ran a vegan bakery.

When their conversation had petered out, West balked at the chat board she'd granted him access to, finding people building morbid spells for things like necromancy and enslavement.

But the other boards had failed him so far and he figured this was the best way to get more information about the demon.

Maybe Kit didn't believe that Mike would be involved in anything like this, but West suspected that he had been. He worried what that meant for Kit and Riley; monsters didn't often go quietly into the night after a brutal murder.

West started a new board, starting a topic about Rithys and saying that he'd come across it in some reading. He typed that he'd read that the demon was about healing or fixing things, but that it didn't seem like something a demon would do. He asked if anyone had more information, then posted it.

He thought the post would get a few bites, even if it was nothing more than people coming out of the woodwork to defend demons. Plenty of people who trifled in darker magics like to say that black magic wasn't any more dangerous than those who practiced more standard forms of the craft, that it all boiled down to the intention of the caster, not the nature of the magic. They generally clammed up when someone pointed out that a curse for giving people cancer really only had one kind of intention.

Witches who fully dedicated themselves to the black arts never bothered to defend themselves and that gave West a lot of pause.

West stared at his computer for a bit, then turned it off. He'd get an email if anyone replied to his post.

The idea of spending the rest of the night hiding in the basement didn't appeal to him, but he didn't want to go upstairs and get an earful of whatever Laurel had thought up since he'd fled down here.

He wished he could skip right to tomorrow.

This time West had been the one to ask Kit somewhere. The more he thought about it, the more the idea felt lame, but he held out hope that Kit would like it.

Tomorrow would tell.

His phone made a sound that it didn't usually make and he looked over to see that Evie had sent him a Facebook message. He'd downloaded the messenger app when he'd been going back and forth with her before; he'd avoided it previously because people who sent him Facebook messages weren't often people he wanted to talk to. He'd always preferred texting because then only people he'd given his number could bother him at all hours of the day.

He dragged his phone over and considered deleting the app. He gave her message a chance and glanced it over. She'd asked why he wanted to get on to that board in the first place. He fed her a half-truth about something he'd found in his grandmother's grimoire, which he sort of regretted because it turned into her asking him a thousand and one questions about the grimoire.

He half-assed the answers then told her he had to go after about ten minutes. He didn't need to get mixed up in any more of this.

Evie took his departure well, telling him to have a great day. Her cheeriness set West on edge; as far as he knew, Evie had never done anything too terrible to anyone, but that had been years ago. She could have started hexing newborn babies for all he knew.

He kind of doubted someone who hexed babies would marry a vegan baker, though.

He stretched and paced around the basement. Part of him wanted to go upstairs, but the larger, louder part of him wondered if he could crawl out through the ground-level window above his bed. The window was about the same size as a cinderblock, so he didn't like the odds.

Around nine, the doorknob jiggled but the lock held. "West," Laurel called, her voice muffled by the door and the distance between his bed and the stairs.

He rolled onto his side, away from the sound of her voice, and continued scrolling through Instagram. Someone he knew in Colorado had found a litter of kittens under their porch and he desperately wanted one.

"West, come on. Let me come down," she called.

He commented that the kittens were adorable and scrunched into a ball, pulling his covers up.

"I want to talk."

The softness of her request tempted him. He sat up, padded over to the bottom of the stairs, and asked, "Talk about what?"

"Talk about whatever's going on with you."

"Nothing's going on."

"West!" she whined. "You're messing around with dark stuff!"

He walked away from the stairs, rifled through his bedside table, and packed a bowl. He cracked the window above his bed and settled on to the futon to watch *The Bridge on the River Kwai*. It was what he'd planned to do on Sunday, though he'd jumped at the chance to make better plans with Kit.

Staying home and smoking alone had lost the broad appeal it had held a year ago, but that didn't mean it wasn't what he did whenever he had no plans and a few extra bucks. He rarely had plans, since all of his friends from college lived out of state, and this was cheaper than going out and having to pay a cover to get in somewhere and for drinks.

Tuesday

WEST WAITED in the basement until Kit texted him that he'd arrived. He'd specifically requested that, not having the guts or the patience to share space with his sister at the moment. When he hurried upstairs and spotted her with her usual bowl of oatmeal, he slowed his pace. He didn't want to look like he'd been flustered.

She'd only take it as a sign of guilt.

When she heard him, she looked up. "Listen, West—"

"I've gotta go." He made a beeline for the door, keeping his pace intentionally steady; he also didn't look at her.

"Westley!" She stood up and smacked her hand on the kitchen table.

He paused. "Unless you're gonna tell me you're fine with me seeing him, I don't want to hear it."

"How could I be fine with it!" she demanded.

"So then I don't want to hear it." He scooted out the front door, hoping that would be the end of it.

She followed him. "I don't want to tell Mom—"

He whirled around, halfway down the steps, and almost fell because of it. He couldn't help the bark of incredulous laughter that escaped. "Tell Mom! I'm fucking twenty-seven, you can't tell my mom on me anymore!"

"Would just listen for a second?"

He continued down the stairs and headed down the walkway. Kit had once again parked in front of the driveway instead of in it. "Why? You guys gonna ground me?" he called over his shoulder.

He saw that she was following him and hurried to get into the car.

Kit moved in and gave him a quick kiss, to which West responded, "You should start driving."

"I don't know where we're going."

"Just start driving," West insisted.

Kit leaned forward a little and peered out the window, his eyes narrowed. "Is that your sister again?"

"Yes, now come on, before she does something."

"Does something? I thought you guys were, uh, you were all Good Witches," Kit said, his cadence carrying the impersonation of Billie Burke as Glinda.

"Would you just drive!"

Laurel had gotten most of the way down the drive and West didn't want to find out what she had to say to Kit.

Kit drove, pulling away, and then glanced towards West with a stupid grin on his face.

"What?" West demanded.

The demon had a laugh in his voice as he said, "No, I just never thought of it before."

"Thought of what?"

"Well, I mean, the Wicked Witches, you know." He sniggered. "The Wicked Witch of the West—"

"Haha, fucking hilarious. Next, you can start quoting lines from *The Princess Bride* at me," West growled.

"Alright, take it easy," Kit soothed. "You gonna tell me where I'm going?"

West pulled up the address on his phone and started the map route. He placed it in the cupholder. "It's still a surprise."

"Oof," Kit said. "I think you meant to say that all cute and playful, but it came out super mean."

"Westley is a stupid name."

"Ahh, it's not so bad," Kit soothed, "It's got panache. Westley. It's sounds kind of dashing."

"Mmm," West grunted.

"Better than Clarence," the demon offered.

"Well, no shit it's better than Clarence. Who the fuck is

named Clarence?" he growled, not sure why he was being so touchy, other than spending the entirety of grade school being known as The Wicked Witch of the West, with a lot of emphasis on the 's' in West.

"Clarence Christopher Reeves," Kit said easily.

West wrinkled his nose, then narrowed his eyes and looked towards Kit. "Clarence?"

"It's sort of grown on me if we're being honest."

Kit was being honest.

He continued, "Mike wanted to give Riley one of those butch names, uh, you know, like Hunter or Gunner. Emmet was in the running for a while, I just about died. Finally, I talked him into Riley 'cause O'Reilly was Mike's mother's maiden name. Still, the kid has a doozy of a name. Riley Sean McAuliffe."

"You talk about him a lot," West pointed out.

Kit made a face. "Well, he's my son, so..."

"No. Mike."

"Oh. Well." Kit shifted. "I think that's normal, right? I mean, we were together for a long time."

West shrugged. He didn't know if it was normal or not, he just knew that whenever Kit brought up Mike there was an odd note in the tone of his voice. Not longing or bitterness, but a pang of some kind.

"And he's Riley's dad. I'm gonna probably have to talk about him for the rest of my life," Kit mentioned, his tone cautious.

"Mhm."

They left it at that.

West's phone directed them to a small museum and Kit turned into the parking lot hesitantly, glancing at West for confirmation.

"This is it," West assured.

"Okay." Kit glanced at the sign, probably not sure what The Walton Museum of Theurgy held for him.

Kit didn't express any dismay or doubt as they walked towards the museum, but West felt the need to tell him, "You're gonna like it, I promise."

"Well, I'm definitely interested," Kit admitted as he eyed the pentagram hanging over the door.

Kit stopped walking, though, before they got inside, staring off towards the road, his brow creased.

"Hey." West tugged on his hand.

"Sorry. I thought...never mind."

West pushed open the door and handed over a ten to the decrepit man working the counter. He was known to every witch child in the area as the Goblin. Rumor had it that he'd turned three hundred a few years ago, but no one would have dared to ask. His counter was littered with skulls, dead things preserved in jars, suspiciously human-looking teeth strung on bits of leather, and old, rusted medical tools.

Kit openly ogled the collection.

The man handed them both a small red admission ticket and looked them over.

The Goblin, who bore a name tag with 'Kalifax' engraved on it, leered at West and asked, "A little old to be playing truth or dare, aren't we, witchboy?"

West's face grew hot. Grown witches sneered at the Walton the way people sneered at haunted houses. Having to cough up five dollars and make it through the Museum was the go-to dare for young witches, though, but always in pairs. Rumor said that lone witches went missing around the Walton family and that their packed, maze of a museum was the perfect trap for an unattended witch boy or girl.

He shoved his ticket into the pocket of his shorts and Kalifax cackled at him.

Kit came up behind him and slung an arm across his chest. "Are you taking me on a spooky date?" he asked, his cheek brushing against West's cheek.

"Yes."

Kit tightened his embrace, pressed a kiss to the side of West's face, then took him by the hand and headed into the gallery.

The Walton Museum of Theurgy, which was little more than a converted farmhouse, had seven gallery rooms spread over two floors; the exhibits were organized into the categories of Preserves, Tools, Literature, Relics, Art, Familiars, and Possessed Objects. Beyond those labels, nothing was systematized. Each room had things packed onto roped-off shelves or laid out in glass display cases.

As a child, he'd tiptoed through the place hand-in-hand with Crissie Petersen, both of them shaking and jumping out of their skin at the slightest sound. They'd been absolutely convinced that buying a ticket was tantamount to signing over their souls.

Now he tilted his head at one of the display cases and realized it was from Ikea.

Kit didn't seem to notice the furniture, though, and walked through the Preserves room with wide-eyed wonder. He peered into each glass jar, cooing over two-headed kittens and fetal pigs.

In Tools, he tried to guess the purpose of each of the instruments on display. Some of his guesses were startlingly accurate and West got the feeling that Kit knew more about old-timey surgical apparatus than the average person. In Literature, he pressed his face close to the displays, almost touching, trying to get a look at the illustrations and passages that lined the yellowed pages.

By the time, they got to the room full of taxidermized Familiars, West had long since gotten over the Museum's dusty, claustrophobic atmosphere. He'd forgotten about having to go home and face his sister. He was too interested in watching Kit gasp and bubble over each grotesque object and dead thing.

Kit was too interested in the displays to notice that West had been taking selfies with him in the background, usually making a face that expressed that Kit was a surprisingly adorable dork.

"Do you *see this?*" Kit demanded in a hushed voice, pulling on West's hand so he would come closer and look at the stuffed wolf that had been set up in the corner. "How come I've never heard of this place?"

"I dunna, did you grow up around here?"

"No, but still, you think someone would have mentioned it."

"You hang out with a lot of witches?" West asked.

Kit didn't answer, but released West's hand and asked, "You broomstick types really had *wolves* as familiars?"

"Sure, but look at the date on it," West suggested.

Kit peered closer to see that the animal had died in the early eighteenth century. "How do you think they got their hands on it?"

"Rumor has it that, that these are their familiars."

"Whose?" Kit straightened up, his brow furrowed, his eyes still on the wolf.

"The Walton family. They're a founding family, you know, for Lowell Falls. Them, the Lowell family, and the Archers."

Kit turned around to look at him. "I'm sorry, the Archers?"

"Distant relations."

"Yeah, no shit, this town was founded in, like, the sixteen-hundreds," Kit pointed out. "Are you telling me I've been paling around with witch royalty?"

West snorted. "Paling around?"

Gone was the open warmth he'd had for their whole trek

through the museum. The aloofness was back, that casual expression that said he hadn't wasted his time thinking about it. "I don't know, we still haven't decided what we're doing."

"Dating?" West offered.

Kit raked his fingers through his hair and didn't quite look at West when he asked, "Exclusively?"

Kit shrugged. "Yeah, I mean, why not?"

" 'Cause if you don't want to—"

"Do you not want to?" West asked.

"No, but you're young. You might have other people you want to see."

West shrugged, wondering which part of that statement was leaving the taste of dishonesty on the air. "I went to college, I sowed my oats," he said, not particularly attached to the lifestyle that involved dating around or hooking up.

"Alright, well."

West waited, somewhat underwhelmed by the response. Kit didn't say anything else, though and they moved into the last room of the Museum.

"Alright, well what?" West asked. When Kit hesitated, West pressed more harshly than he should have, "I don't give a shit if you want to see other people so you might as well say that you do."

He walked away from Kit and went over to look at one of the supposedly possessed dolls. It sat on a shelf with a dozen other dolls, including one sad 80s Barbie with all its hair shorn off.

The demon remained in the center of the room, his eyes following West as he circled around the room. "It's *not* that."

More relieved than he should have been, West asked, "Then what is it?"

"You're young," Kit repeated.

"I'm twenty-seven."

Kit winced.

"That's, like, almost thirty," West said, not sure why he wanted to sound older than he was. He moved away from the dolls and went over to a steering wheel that had been propped up against a cabinet. He couldn't tell if it was part of the display or being used to hold the cabinet door closed.

A headache pinched right behind his eyes. He should have eaten something for breakfast, but Laurel had been hanging around in the kitchen trying to talk to him.

"I don't know, I just...I don't know if we're looking for the same thing in a relationship," Kit explained, not exactly sounding happy about it.

" 'Cause you've got a kid and I'm basically unemployed?" West guessed.

The demon grimaced. "Sort of."

"Then why the fuck did you give me your number?" West asked, turning his back on a display case full of Precious Memories figurines.

"I thought you were cute."

"And you were looking for, what, something casual?" West honestly didn't know where he got the balls to make these kinds of accusations when he'd been planning on hooking up with Kit in an alley. A wave of lightheadedness swept over him and he adjusted his stance to keep his balance.

"No." Kit shook his head and took a half a step towards West.

"You thought, oh, here's some dumb Crunchy Granola. Some gym bunny, wanna-be hipster, he seems gay," West accused, "I bet I can get him to suck my dick."

"Now you're being mean." Kit's cool exterior slipped, showing a hint of...of what?

West couldn't figure out the expression on his face. He didn't like it, whatever it was. He wanted Kit to go back to marveling over the displays, his face lit up with delight at the grotesque and abnormal sights. "I took you on a spooky date," he reminded.

He hadn't eaten in a while. Since lunch yesterday, now that he thought of it. He hadn't ever ventured back upstairs after his non-fight with Laurel.

"I told my sister."

"You what?"

"I told my sister," West repeated, somewhere between wanting to cry and needing to sit down. He rubbed his eyes. Maybe he should have skipped his run that morning.

"What'd she say?" Kit asked.

"I don't know, I hid in the basement for the rest of the night. Listen, I feel like shit, can we get out of here?" Suddenly West could feel the eyes of every possessed doll, figurine, and painting on him and possession didn't seem like such a crock anymore.

Kit studied him for a moment, concern showing plainly on his face. "Yeah, alright, let's go." He put a hand on West's arm. "I've got to pick up Riley in a little while anyway."

"I'm sorry, I just...Maybe I need some air or something." He needed to eat.

"What doesn't feel good?" Kit asked as they walked. "Does your head hurt?"

"Holy shit, I'm not five."

"Did you drink any water today?"

Begrudgingly, he answered, "No."

"What did you have for breakfast?" Kit asked, not dissuaded by West's tone.

"Nothing."

"Okay, dummy, there's your problem. Come on, we drove by a Dunkin on the way here." Kit glanced at his phone.

"No, it's fine."

"No, it's lunchtime," Kit said firmly. "You can join the sacred ranks of people who are allowed to eat in my car."

West gave up protesting.

Once he'd housed a breakfast sandwich, he felt better physically, though his recovery was tinged with embarrassment. Skipping meals was stupid, he knew better than that.

"So, uh, West, I know I was kind of giving you a hard time before," Kit began.

"I deserved it."

"No, you didn't. I've got some stuff going on, stuff with...well, you know, never mind," the demon said. "But I'm sorry. About...you know."

"I don't know."

"Me neither, not really. I think...I don't know, this is the closest I've gotten to anything in a long time. I don't know if I'm nervous or what."

"That's not gonna hold up in court," West told him.

Kit huffed. "Fine, alright, how about I'm fucking terrified?"

"There you go." Truth, two layers. Kit was terrified of what could happen between them, yes, but there was more to it than that.

Kit scowled and fixed his eyes on the road, as though staring down the pavement would make West disappear.

"I am, too," West said, staring at the pile of garbage on his lap. He crumpled up the bag and let out a sigh. "This is...you know, it's weird. But I *like* being around you."

"Hashtag same," the demon whispered.

West's head jerked up, not sure he'd heard right; laughter jumped out of him. He reached over and put a hand on Kit's leg, relieved when Kit took his hand. "So, let's date. Exclusive and everything."

"Sounds good."

"And maybe we could find time to sleep together again."

Kit chuckled, though the laugh was tinged with something. Nervousness, maybe, or scandal. "I'll try to schedule a time for that, too."

"You can add it to your list of Friday chores."

The demon rolled his eyes.

"Or is once a month all you can manage at your advanced age?" West teased.

"I could pull over right now and show you what I can manage," Kit growled.

His voice sent a ripple of heat and need through West and he said, "Ooh, don't threaten me with a good time."

"I swear if I didn't have to pick up my kid..." the demon grumbled.

West didn't know about that, but he'd be willing to put it to the test sometime. He'd grown up around here, knew all the places where people could park safely away from prying eyes. He thought about sharing that with Kit but decided to save it for another time. He'd already made him late to pick up his kid once.

"Do you want to tell me about the other stuff that's going on?" West asked.

"No."

West raised an eyebrow, waiting for him to remember that lying was useless.

"Not really," the demon amended. "I feel like I'm losing it."

"Never a good sign," West said.

"It's that...you know how I've been trying to figure out if there's any clues to who killed Mike? Like, if he knew her on Facebook or anything?"

"Sure."

Kit paused for a long time, a myriad of expressions flowing over his face, before he settled on, "I don't know, it's just getting to me. Every time I see a brunette with her hair pulled back..." He sighed and tapped his knuckles against the steering wheel. "I can't stop thinking about if *that's* the woman who bashed his head in before he could even un-holster his gun."

"Kit..."

"I had to go pick up Riley, you know, when they found Mike, and the kid was having a hard enough time as it was. I really made sure Rye didn't see anything on the way out but, god help me, I fucking looked, West. I couldn't help it. I mean, he was so *strong*, I didn't believe anyone could hurt him. There was no way he could be dead."

West reached over and put his hand over Kit's.

"He was pretty fucking dead, though. Don't think I've ever seen anything deader." The demon let out a teary laugh. "I'm sorry, look at me, I'm a mess." He took his hand back and ground the meat of his palm into his eyes.

"You are allowed to feel sad about things, you know, that's not being a mess," West pointed out, hoping it came across as helpful instead of snarky.

"I'm sick of being sad."

"I know a spell for that."

"Oh, yeah? Not from that spooky book of yours," Kit said.

"No."

"Good, 'cause I don't want you to go cursing me by accident or anything."

West snorted. "I'd have to be a pretty terrible witch to curse you by accident."

"I don't want you to curse me on purpose, either," Kit pointed out.

"Good thing I like you, then."

Kit dropped him off in front of the house, giving him a sweet, slow kiss goodbye that promised they'd find time to do more sometime soon. West floated inside, giddy and forgetting to worry about what Laurel would have to say.

LAUREL CAME home early to find West lounging on the couch watching HGTV. He'd been going back and forth with Evie a little. Someone had sent him a PM on the board and he'd double-checked with her to see if the person was legit; the Community was small and the section that practiced the dark arts was even smaller.

She assured him that polywitchgirl88 had a good reputation and then asked him what he was trying to figure out, anyway. He parsed out a few details and was in the middle of telling her about a sketchy spell of his grandmother's for dealing with barking neighborhood dogs when Laurel came in.

West glanced towards his sister and debated whether or not he should greet her. He decided that it would be better to set things off on a good note. "Hi, Laurel."

In response, she came into the living room and dropped the grimoire on the coffee table from a height sufficient to make the table rattle.

He sat up quickly enough that his phone slid off his chest and thudded to the floor.

"We need to talk," Laurel announced.

He grabbed his phone and buried it in his pocket before she could glimpse the messages he'd been sending. "You went through my room."

"You *stole that,*" she countered.

He rubbed the back of his neck. "Yeah, but—"

"There's no but, West! You *stole from your own mother!*" she cried.

He winced and didn't think asking her to lower her voice would help his case. "I just needed to look something up."

"And you didn't ask because...?"

West huffed and made himself stand. "Because I knew you'd react like this if I did."

She snatched up the grimoire and shook it in his direction. "Fine, alright. What could you possibly need out of that book? What was so important you've been lying to me and Mom?"

"A, uh, a demon sigil."

"A demon...! A demon sigil!" she shouted at him. "You know what those are for, don't you?"

"Summoning demons, yeah, but—"

"How could you *possibly*—"

"Laurel, shut up! Let me finish," he barked.

She turned even redder than she had been before but said nothing.

"I'm not trying to summon a demon, alright? I think...I'm pretty sure that this Mike guy did and, you know, I'm trying to figure it all out."

"What Mike guy?"

"Kit's ex."

She put one hand on her hip and gave him a pitying look, which was worse than shouting. "He's got you digging around in his ex's business?"

He sighed and didn't even know where to start explaining things. He didn't even feel that Laurel was entitled to an explanation about anything anyway. "This is kind of between me and him, Laurel. If I'd wanted you to know, I would have told you."

She let out a sigh and fixed her eyes on him. He could have sworn they were glistening with tears. "You've got to end this. Whatever's going on, it's got to stop."

"That's not gonna happen." Not when just a kiss from the other man had made him so giddy, not when it hurt to see Kit's face flicker with worry, not when Kit and Riley needed someone to figure this out before one of them got hurt.

"You're getting mixed up in bad stuff, West..."

He pulled in a long breath and tuned her out, waiting for the end of her diatribe. By the time she'd finished, he'd lost track of all her accusations. Carefully, he told her, "I'm not mixed up in anything. I'm not summoning demons or casting hexes. It's research and we're dating. That's it. None of this has to be a big deal."

"West, please," she pleaded.

He shook his head.

"Then get out of my house."

He went cold all over and at first, all he could do was stare at her. "Are you serious?" he asked, even though there was no trace of a lie in her voice.

She nodded.

"I pay rent," he protested weakly.

"You could pay me a million dollars and I wouldn't care. You're not gonna bring that kind of stuff into my *home*."

"Laurel—"

"No, that's...that's absolutely final, West." She sniffled and fat tears rolled down her freckled cheeks. "You've got until the end of the week." Her voice strained, thick and low, like it hurt her to do this.

His usual move here would be to call his mother and get her to talk sense into Laurel or ask if he could crash at her place. Somehow, he didn't think his mother would be welcoming him with open arms right now.

He'd give his sister a day to cool off, he decided.

And if she couldn't, then it was better that they had some distance between them.

He headed towards the basement, impressed with his stoicism until he sat down on the futon and started to shake, first his hands, then all over. He curled up and shoved his face into a decorative pillow, not crying, but weeping.

He hadn't cried like this in years, not even when Danny had dumped him. He'd known it was coming, no matter how much he'd lied to himself about it. Getting dumped had been nothing, the predictable end of something that had died ages ago.

The last time he'd cried like this he had been balled up in the corner of the men's bathroom at a swanky restaurant on their third anniversary. He'd told Danny that he loved him, nothing more than one of those casual affectionate exchanges they had periodically. It wasn't a grand announcement and he hadn't expected anything more than a comfortable reassurance.

Instead, he'd gotten the coldest lie he'd ever felt, a "You too, babe," that had sounded exactly the same as all the other times

Danny had said it.

After he'd sobbed himself dry and swaddled himself in his favorite pajamas, he spent the next few hours numbly scrolling through apps on his phone. None of it registered. He kept returning to his instinct to call his mother, but he didn't think he could endure the sight of her being as upset as Laurel had been.

In the back of his mind, he wanted to call Kit, but he didn't let himself even settle on that idea. They hadn't even gone on enough dates to call themselves a couple and he had no idea what he expected Kit to even do. He couldn't help and West had absolutely zero plans to infringe on any hospitality the demon might offer him.

Around midnight, he'd come out of his funk enough to make some dinner and finally read the PM that polywitchgirl88 had sent. It was an offer to email him a PDF of a book entitled *Enchiridion daemonis*, a book she said she'd found at the estate sale of Risalda Timberton when she'd died about a decade ago. If half the rumors about Riz Timberton were true, then the country was lucky that she'd had to compete with Marilyn Monroe and Jackie O. for the affections of JFK. Otherwise, they probably would have had an Enchantress Queen instead of a First Lady.

They also might have won Vietnam.

He accepted, sending her his email address along with an overlong and falsely cheerful thank-you note. Once he'd started typing, he hadn't been able to stop. She hadn't responded by the time he'd gone to sleep.

Not that the uneasy haze of dreams he settled into could be properly called sleep. He woke every so often to toss around, paw at his blankets, and grumpily burrow back into his pillows.

A few minutes shy of seven, his phone rang. He ignored it, rolling over and pulling his covers over his head before he realized that this was not just another nightmare about being trapped in a cubicle with a dozen bleating phones.

West dragged over his phone and squinted at it. When he saw that Kit was the one calling, he answered with a bleary, "Hello?"

"I woke you up."

"Yes." Hearing Kit's voice over the phone felt wrong somehow, it felt like seeing a home video of a relative who'd died before he'd been born.

"I'm sorry, listen, I..." The demon let out a sigh. "I didn't know who else to call."

"Is everything okay?"

"I, I mean, can I get your opinion on something? Like, if I sent you a picture, you'd tell me what you saw?" he asked.

"Yeah, of course," West rushed to answer, not liking the waver in Kit's voice.

"Alright, let me know when you get it. I just, I was giving Rye a bath last night and, well...I don't know, he had these...marks on his arms."

Something slick and ugly wormed its way into West's gut. It coiled there, waiting.

"And, uh, I'm gonna send you a picture. I just want you to tell me I'm not crazy," Kit explained.

West's phone buzzed a few seconds later and he opened the message to see a mottled grayish pattern over the thin, round arm of a child. Another picture came a moment later showing the same marks, this time darker but still indistinct.

They looked like bruises, not the purple ones to be found on a living person but the gray-black ones that decorated the ghosts in horror movies. West worried that Kit had sent him a picture of a corpse, but the thought dissipated after West sat up and looked at the pictures more closely.

"West?" came Kit's voice, hushed and tight.

"Yeah, sorry, I was just looking. That's...is he feeling alright?" West ventured.

"I mean, yeah, no fever, no cough, or anything like that. But I mean, the second picture is from this morning."

"They got darker for sure," West agreed. "I don't know what these are. You've got to take him to the doctor."

"And tell them what? That he just woke up like that?" Kit asked, panic making his tone sharp. "Everyone already thinks I'm a shitty dad."

"Tell the truth. You don't know what happened. Maybe it's an allergic reaction or something," West soothed. He didn't honestly know what those marks could mean. He hoped Kit would find some medical solution; the other option, the one involving what Mike had done to their son, made West feel sick.

"Okay."

"Let me know if he's okay. If you need anything."

"Yeah, I will. Thanks."

West stared at his phone, rubbed his face, and decided to skip his run that morning. He slogged through a shower and danced around his sister in the kitchen.

He fought the urge to retreat to the basement. "Laurel."

She didn't look at him. "Mmm?"

"You're really serious about this."

"Yes."

"The end of the week?" he asked.

"That's what I said," she answered.

He managed to keep most of the whine out of his voice when he asked, "Can you at least give me time to find a job? A place to go?"

That got her attention, drawing her gaze toward him. "I said the end of the week."

"I'm not asking you to let me stay, I'm asking you to give me enough time to get my shit together," he pointed out, trying to keep his voice even. "That's it."

She didn't answer.

" 'Cause, you know, I'm not exactly chomping at the bit to stay here if this is how you're gonna be about things."

"Why don't you ask your new *boyfriend* to help you out?" she sneered.

"Can you not be a bitch about this?" he demanded.

He didn't have any idea where he would go if he had to be out of here by Friday. A motel, probably, he had enough money for a few days. His skin crawled at the idea of being without a permanent residence.

Homeless, he reminded himself. He'd be homeless.

And unemployed.

"You know I don't have anywhere else to go," he reminded in a last-ditch effort.

She stood up straighter but didn't get the chance to answer.

The doorbell rang.

They both looked over.

West caught a glimpse of a tattooed arm and tousled hair through the window. He pounced on the door before Laurel could. He scrambled out on to the porch, ready to ask Kit what the hell was going on.

Then he saw Riley standing close beside his father, stark, black symbols winding up his arms and across his throat and face.

"It's not an allergy," Kit told him.

"Yeah, I guess not," West conceded.

Riley, to his credit, didn't seem concerned. He had his stuffed bunny clamped securely under one arm and his other hand wobbling in the air beside his chest. He bobbed his head from side to side every so often.

"I didn't know where else to go, I can't take him anywhere like this," Kit admitted quietly.

"No."

It would be one thing to bring a kid with a rash or some weird bruising to the doctor, it would be something else entirely to tow around a preschooler covered with tattoos.

West glanced towards Laurel, who glowered at them through the window. She probably only had a view of his back and Kit's profile, but he could feel the heat of her gaze anyway.

He didn't have any other choice. He couldn't turn either of them away. He had no idea what to do about this but figured he must have had more people to ask for advice. "Come in, I'll make tea or something. You want something to eat?"

Kit didn't answer but followed solemnly into the house. Riley scooted along in his father's wake.

"Are you fucking kidding!" Laurel demanded, rushing over to the door as if she meant to physically push Kit back outside.

Kit put up a wary hand to ward off whatever she might do, positioned himself between her and Riley, and frowned, his eyes flicking between West and Laurel.

Riley babbled several lines that seemed to be from a Scooby-Doo episode to himself.

Laurel took half a step back, peered at the boy, then rounded on West, hissing, "What the hell are you mixed up in?"

"This is Kit," West said. "And his son, Riley."

"Are you kidding?" she asked.

West shook his head. "Why would I make that up?

She jabbed him in the chest. "No, I mean, how stupid are you, West? That's a *human* child. Covered in sigils. With a demon."

Several answers ran through West's mind, none of them nice, so he held his tongue and nodded for Kit to come towards the basement. "Come on, I guess we'll hang out down here."

Laurel watched them go, then stepped between Kit and Riley. "I don't know what you're up to—"

"You're gonna want to move," Kit warned.

At the same time, West insisted, "Laurel, don't."

Riley froze, staring up at Laurel.

Kit took a step forward and Laurel put out a hand to block him. "I'm not about to let you—"

Riley dodged around Laurel and grasped on to his father's leg, clinging so hard West was surprised he hadn't started climbing his way up.

He didn't have to because Kit scooped him up and settled him on his hip. He wound both his arms around the child, one hand cradling the back of his head. Riley had buried his face against his father's shoulder.

West put one hand on Kit's arm. "Go on downstairs."

Kit didn't move and West gave him a little bit of a pull. His eyes still fixed on Laurel, Kit took a slow step back.

West opened the basement door and saw him through. "I'll be down in a minute," West assured.

Kit went and Laurel moved in close to West. "You saw that, didn't you? The way he was looking at me."

"You're kidding, right?" West asked. "Can you imagine someone pulling a stunt like that with Mom?"

"You can't really believe that's his son, West, you're not stupid."

"I don't know, he goddamn picked him up from preschool the other day and usually they don't let random strangers waltz on in and take their pick of the kids," West told her. "Where's the grimoire?"

"I'm not giving it to you."

West didn't think there was any point in arguing with her. He headed to his room, locking the door behind him.

He found Kit sitting on the futon with Riley in his lap.

"Sorry about her."

Kit ruffled Riley's hair and kissed the top of his head. "You pointy hats..." the demon grumbled.

"I know," West said. Not too long ago, though, he would have made the same kind of assumptions about Kit. The runes all over the boy didn't help. He rubbed the back of his neck. "He's got those all over?"

"Big one on his chest."

"What's it look like?"

Kit patted Riley on the leg. "Hop up, buddy." Riley stood up and Kit settled his hands on the boy's shoulders. "You remember West, right?"

Riley glanced towards West and nodded.

"Alright. He's my friend and he's...he's gonna help us figure out what all these silly marks are doing on you," Kit said, his voice sweet and calm.

Riley looked at his hands.

"You know when you go to the doctor and you have to get undressed? West, he's kind of like a doctor. He's gonna take a look at you, okay?"

West wasn't anything like a doctor but knew better than to point it out. Pretending that West was a doctor had to be smarter than bringing a child into the basement and having him get undressed for a stranger.

"What's like a doctor?" Riley asked.

"He, uh, you know how Daddy fixes booboos and makes the nightlight?"

"Use the magic."

Kit nodded. "Exactly. West is like a doctor for magic things. He's called a witch. He knows about magic, about spells and fixing things. More than I do. Can you show him the big mark on your chest?"

Kit removed his hands from his son's shoulders. Riley handed over his stuffed rabbit, pulled his shirt over his head, and turned around to show West the spiky, angular sigil stamped on his chest.

West hardly needed to look at it to know what it was. He'd spent plenty of time staring at that exact sigil. He moved past the other two and emptied out his bedside table to find the suncatcher he'd hidden within.

Once he'd found it, he undid the knots and handed it over to Kit. "So I know you didn't want to hear about it before..."

Kit turned the suncatcher over in his hands, his eyes darting between then sigil on the catcher and the mark on his son's chest. He said nothing.

"Go ahead and get dressed," West told Riley. He didn't need to see any more of the sigils. He couldn't read them, anyway.

The boy pulled on his shirt and took his rabbit.

Kit glanced towards his son, then made eye contact with West. They needed to talk and couldn't do it with Riley present. Talking about murders and curses in earshot of a preschooler was bad form.

It had to be a curse.

"Laurel's got to go to work in a bit," West told him. "We can go upstairs then."

Kit nodded. "Yeah."

Riley tapped his father on the leg. "Daddy, I'm hungry."

Kit glanced towards West and Riley followed his gaze. "You

like pancakes?" West asked.

"Yes."

"I'll make pancakes."

"Now?" the boy asked.

West checked the time. "Ten minutes."

"Set a timer?" Riley asked.

"Uh, sure." West grabbed his phone and set a timer. He showed it to the boy.

Riley nodded and climbed onto the futon beside his father. He leaned his head against Kit's arm. "I just can't *be* with you like this anymore."

West had been putting everything back into his bedside table. He looked over to Kit, head tilted to the side.

"He just says things sometimes," Kit explained.

Riley looked up at his father and whispered, "Quiet voice?"

"No," Kit told him. "You're fine. Go ahead."

Riley nestled back against his father and continued to say things to himself.

When the timer went off, they all startled. West went upstairs first to see if Laurel had left and once he confirmed that she had, he called for the other two to come up.

He rummaged through the cabinets, found that they had no pancake mix, and tugged down a cookbook from the shelf.

"You need help?" Kit asked.

"You know where anything is?" West asked.

"No."

"Then I don't need help."

The demon frowned.

Riley ran his hands up and down his father's forearm and whispered to himself.

West gathered the ingredients he needed but glanced back over his shoulder at one point when he heard the other two carrying out a full conversation lifted from an episode of Scooby-Doo. His attention had been drawn not by the conversation so much as the sound of Kit doing a spot-on Shaggy impersonation.

"Jinkies," West chimed weakly. He'd felt the urge to say something, to somehow be part of what they were doing. He didn't know if it was his childhood love of Scooby-Doo or a more recent affection for Kit that had moved him.

They both looked at him.

Riley waved a hand at him, a motion that West understood to

be a gesture of negation. "No Velma."

"Sorry." West felt his face grow hot. He turned back to the counter and dug through one of the drawers to find a measuring cup.

He felt someone tug on his shirt and turned to see Riley standing beside him. "No Velma."

"Yeah, uh. Sorry."

"Freddie."

"What?"

"Looks like we have another mystery on our hands," Riley said.

West stared at the boy then looked to Kit, who nodded encouragingly. "Looks like we have another mystery on our hands," West echoed in a hollow imitation of Freddie Jones.

"Good saying it," the child praised.

"Thanks." West didn't know what to do with that compliment, so he checked the cabinet to see if they had the right ingredients, then asked, "You, uh...you like chocolate chip pancakes?"

He nodded.

"What about banana pancakes?"

The boy's face contorted. He shook his head as emphatically as West imagined he would if he'd been offered worm pancakes.

"Okay."

"I don't wanna try it."

"Okay," West agreed.

"I don't wanna try it," Riley repeated, slightly more distressed than the first time.

West wondered if it would have been better not to say anything at all. "I wasn't gonna make you."

"No banana pancakes?"

"No," West promised.

Riley asked, "Just chocolate chip?"

"Sure."

"I don't want banana pancakes," Riley insisted.

"Okay." West glanced towards Kit. "What about you?"

"I'll eat anything," Kit admitted.

"No bananas," Riley reminded anxiously.

"Rye," Kit called, though he sounded more amused than anything. "He said no bananas. It's fine."

"It's fine," Riley echoed.

"Yeah," his father assured.

Riley left West's side to return to his father, lifting his arms wordlessly. Kit scooped him up and gave him a squeeze. Riley giggled and West wondered if the two of them were always this deeply, heartwarmingly adorable together.

Probably not, he decided. All families had their ugly moments.

He changed his mind, though, when Kit pressed a kiss to his son's cheek and Riley wrapped his arms around the demon's neck. He couldn't imagine a single truly ugly moment between the two of them. Unhappy or disagreeable ones he could imagine, but not one of those hideous fights that always seemed to break out in grocery stores or restaurants.

Riley grew bored of standing around in the kitchen soon enough and West directed the two of them towards the living room.

RILEY SAT on the floor of the living room, staring into Mipsy's hutch. He'd noticed her on his way to the TV and had bobbed on his toes with delight, crowing, "A rabbit, Daddy!"

Kit and West had gone to the kitchen, to talk and to cook.

"Have you ever seen anything like it before?" Kit asked. "The marks."

"No, but, well, I don't usually mess with this kind of magic."

Kit rubbed his face.

"Listen, he's gonna be fine," West assured. He eyed the last pancake and waited to flip it.

"You don't know that."

West reached over and placed a hand on Kit's arm. "We're going to figure this out, alright?"

Kit pulled his arm back and shook his head. "Someone's following me."

The abrupt confession stalled West's trail of thought and he struggled to ask, "What?"

"Short, sturdy. Dark hair. Hanging around in front of my house."

West couldn't help but ask, "You have a house?"

"Is that your takeaway from this?" the demon demanded, his voice somewhat strangled.

"My takeaway is that I need to work a spell," West said. "I just can't imagine you in a house, though."

He flipped the pancake.

"Where'd you think I lived?" Kit asked.

"I don't know, a crypt." West straightened up. "The thing about this spell...It's for a location, not a person."

"Alright," Kit said, unsure and his brow slightly creased.

"There's no good in hiding at your place if she's already been there," West clarified. "So..." He looked around the kitchen, trying to remember if they had everything he needed for the spell. "Laurel's kicking me out. I'll hide you here for now, but you can't stay for long. It'll buy you time to find somewhere else."

"She's kicking you out?"

"Mmm." West went to the cabinet and rummaged around. He took his book from the kitchen shelf and double-checked what they had against the spell. "I've got to run up the street, get some herbs."

Hezzie would have what he needed.

Kit nodded.

He paused as he headed towards the door. He put a hand on Kit's shoulder. "It's a good spell, it works."

"How do you know?"

" 'Cause I basically ran a bodega out of my dorm in college and the RAs never so much as sniffed around."

Kit let out a quiet chuckle and put his hand over West's. "Here I was thinking you were such a nice little witch."

West leaned in to give him a kiss, quick and quiet. "I'll be right back. Have some pancakes."

He jogged up the street to Hezzie's and rapped on her door. She would be awake at this hour, he knew. He often saw her out walking her scruffy little mutt when he went for his morning run.

She told him to take whatever he needed and declined his offer to pay. She watched him harvest the herbs.

"What are you hiding?" she asked, one drawn-on eyebrow raised.

"Ahh, it's a secret, Hezzie, that's why I'm hiding it."

"You might want to hide that car, then, too," she pointed out.

He bit back a laugh and rushed home just as quick as he'd gone.

The spell was quick work. It had been a while since he'd cast it, but years ago he'd practically had the thing memorized. Salt, a bit of wormwood, a bit of amaranth. Black candles with the right runes carved into the sides.

Kit watched him prepare, his mouth tight.

"You gonna look at me like that the whole time I work it, too?" West asked.

"Sorry, just...I've never seen anyone do this kind of magic before."

"Never?"

Kit shook his head. "Witchy stuff...I don't know, it always creeped me out."

West set down the candle he carved and demanded, "Creeped you out?"

The demon shrugged. "I don't know, I've seen the shit you guys put in spells."

West snorted, finished his preparations, and wished he'd asked Hezzie to help. The spell didn't need a second, but it never hurt to have more hands on deck. He looked over Kit, wondering if the innate magic inside him would do the trick.

Magic was magic, no matter where it came from. All different ways of tapping into that same force that tied the worlds and their pieces together.

"What?" the demon asked.

"Come help me."

Kit shook his head. "I'm not a witch."

"Nope." West held out his hand palm up.

The demon eyed West's hand for a moment, then sighed and took it.

West tugged him closer. "All you have to do is say what I say. And say it like you mean it," West told him.

"I..."

West turned the opened spell book towards him and tapped the page. "It's all right here."

Kit licked his lips then nodded. "Alright. Yeah." He squared his shoulders and started down the book like it was a curled rattlesnake.

They lit the candles and began the spell, reading together. Kit's voice evened out after a few lines and as West drew down the magic he needed to work the spell, he felt power flowing out of Kit, easy as turning on a faucet. More than just the spark that most people had inside them, more than the lingering flame that burned inside witches and let them tap into the world's energy.

The spell concluded as spells always did, with a sense of emptiness and finality, and not without any fireworks or thunderous confirmations that the universe had accepted their intentions.

"That's it?" Kit asked.

"That's it."

The demon's grip on his tightened. "Don't feel any different."

"Course you don't, spell wasn't on you," West told him. "Come help me rearrange the garage, we've got to hide your car."

Kit looked to Riley, who'd scooted a little closer to Mipsy's hutch. He had a dribble of syrup on his chin and a fork clutched in one hand.

"There's nothing for him to get into."

"Except a kitchen full of knives and dangerous appliances."

West snorted. "Fine, I'll be back. Give me your keys."

The demon handed over the keys without hesitation.

It took West about half an hour to have everything arranged so the SUV could fit inside.

With that done, he returned inside and brought his laptop upstairs. Not wanting to seem rude, he told Kit, "I've, uh, someone sent me a book, I'm gonna look through it and see what else I can find about this Rithys."

"Anything I can do to help?" Kit asked.

"No. Make yourself comfortable."

"Until your sister gets home."

West sighed. "Yeah. Until then."

"And how long are you here until?"

"Listen, it's not anything you need to worry about," West assured. He went to sit on the couch and eyed Riley, wondering how long the kid could sit in front of the rabbit hutch. Every so often he'd start waggling his hands in the air beside his head, take a bite of pancake, or say something to himself, but other than that, his attention was glued to Mipsy as she snuffled around.

"I can't help feeling like it's my fault," Kit said.

"No."

"I gave you a hard time about—"

"Kit, come on, we've got other stuff to worry about. Laurel being a bigot is...you know, it's annoying but it's not the end of the world," West assured, hoping he didn't sound as full of shit as he felt. He didn't know where he would go on Friday. "And I don't want to talk about it."

The demon nodded.

West handed him the remote and turned on his laptop. He

opened up the *Enchiridion daemonis* and combed through it until he found the section on Rithys. If the book could be trusted, she was a Hell-born demon, which meant she was descended from the creatures that Satan had created to populate his realm. References to her went back thousands of years and she had a reputation for preying on those who'd been crippled or struck with some kind of debilitating illness. The cost of her services tended to be high.

And non-negotiable.

"Uh. Kit?"

Kit looked away from the TV he hadn't really been watching. "Yeah?"

"Mike, he, um..."

"What?" Kit prompted when West struggled to find the right words.

West glanced at Riley and felt awful for what he had to ask. He nodded towards the kitchen, not sure how much attention Riley was paying to either of them but not wanting to risk it.

Kit took the empty plates and followed him in.

Once in the kitchen, Kit waited for a bit as West tried to find the right words, then asked, "What?"

"So, you kind of made it sound like Mike, you know, wasn't exactly thrilled to have a, uh, you know, a kid with problems."

"He doesn't have *problems*, he has a developmental disorder," Kit growled. The plates clattered in the sink as he deposited them none too gently.

"Sorry," West mumbled, his veins flooded with ice. "I, just...I'm sorry, I know..." He dug his teeth into his lower lip, not sure why it hurt so much to have Kit look at him like that.

"It's not a problem, *he's* not a problem."

"No, no, of course not, that's not what I mean to say," West hurried to say, praying that Kit couldn't hear the waver in his voice. "It isn't, I just...I wasn't thinking."

He drew in a breath and Kit continued to glower at him.

"I'm sorry," West whispered. He'd meant to say it strong and clear so Kit would know he meant it. He lost control of his mouth and blathered, "I don't think that, I just, I don't know...I don't know. I'm sorry."

Kit glared for a moment longer, then his face softened. He let out a sigh. "It's alright."

"I'm such a shithead."

"You're not a shithead," Kit assured.

"Still. I'm sorry."

"It's fine, I just, I get bent out of shape about it easy." The demon rubbed his nose and admitted, "Mike and I used to have this conversation at least once a week. Except for the part where he admitted he was wrong and apologized. And the part where it was a conversation and not a fight. It was always bad when we had to go to PPTs and those kinds of things."

"A what?"

"It's a meeting when we have to go over goals and all that shit. Mike always...he pushed for these goals that were just impossible. He had this idea that Riley...that he was like this on purpose. That he was...bad 'cause I was soft on him, that he could be squeezed and mashed and molded into being normal. Into being a kid that could, I don't know...who wanted to play catch or whatever fucking heteronormative father-son shit Mike had bought into."

"And you?" West asked.

"I just wanted him to be able to tell me what was wrong when he was upset and not hit himself in the head so much. Or hit other people."

"Oh." He didn't know what to do with that information.

"Which, you know, I will give that place credit, they helped out with that a lot. Now I can see him going to a regular kindergarten next year. Obviously, he'll still need services, but I don't think he needs to be outplaced."

West nodded. "I think Mike made a deal with this Rithys creature. To, uh..." West hesitated, not wanting to misspeak again. "To do what *he* thought would be fixing Riley."

"He's dead."

West chewed on a nail, then explained, "Yeah, but the deal was already struck. A deal's a deal. If the demon got whatever she wanted from him, then she's gonna hold up her end of the deal."

"How do I stop it?"

"I don't know," West admitted, then hurried to add, "Not yet. But I'll find a way. There's got to be something."

Without warning, Kit closed the distance between then and wrapped his arms around West. "I can't let anything happen to him."

"I know."

The demon tightened his grip, then stepped back. He wiped at his eyes, then cleared his throat.

"Kit, it's gonna be okay."

He shook his head.

West drew him close, cradling the demon's face in his hands. "It will. I just need to figure out how. Okay?"

Kit shook his head again. His chest heaved as he drew in quick breaths.

"It will, go on, say it. It's gonna be okay," West soothed.

The other man pulled away, his hands trembling when he swept one through his hair. He patted himself down, searching for something. He drew out a pack of cigarettes and struggled to free one, his fingers trembling. "I'll be right back. Can you keep an eye on him?"

"Stay on the porch."

Kit went and West approached Riley. He settled beside him in front of Mipsy's hutch. "I can let her out if you want."

Riley didn't answer at first and the answer that did come didn't make sense. It was another line from the opening theme of Scooby-Doo.

"Riley."

This time the boy looked at him. "What?"

"You want to hold her?"

He waved his hand as if to fend off the idea.

"She's soft."

He shook his head.

"What if I just hold her and you can pet her?"

That, the boy consented to with a quiet nod.

West took Mipsy out of her hutch and settled her onto his lap. "You can give her a pet on the side, nice and gentle."

Riley reached out with a tentative hand, one which he had kept fastidiously free of syrup, and barely brushed Mipsy's fur with his fingertips. A few moments later, he tried again, this time running his fingers through the rabbit's fur.

"Riley, uh, you know the marks on you?"

The boy nodded.

"Have you ever seen them before?"

"Hang it."

West frowned. "What?"

"Hang it inna window," the boy said. Then his face puckered. "Don't tell Daddy. It's a secret."

"Don't tell him what?"

"About the cure to make me be good."

West bit back a swear, vaguely floored that Mike had told his son that he needed a cure to be good. "Do you know what the cure was?"

Riley shook his head. "She would come and take...take the...I don't know."

"Okay, that's alright."

"It's a secret. You promise too?"

"Sure thing." He returned Mipsy to her hutch and secured the door. Kit hadn't come back inside yet. "You want to play a game?"

"What game?" the boy asked suspiciously, as though West had offered him boiled fish guts instead.

"You know to play go fish?"

Riley shook his head.

"It's easy, I'll teach you."

"No thanks."

"Yeah, it's fun," West insisted. The boy looked at him warily, so West did the same thing his mother had always done when he hadn't wanted to try something new. "Try it first before you say no."

Riley didn't protest so West dug up a deck of cards and showed him how to play.

When Kit came inside a while later, puffy-eyed and reeking of cigarettes, West was deeply embroiled in the game. The demon sat on the floor with them and, with no hesitation, Riley crawled into his father's lap and told him what cards he had.

West tried to keep a straight face.

"He can hear you, you know," Kit told his son.

"Hear you?" the boy echoed.

"Yeah, everything you just said, now he knows what cards you have," Kit explained with a small smile.

The boy stared, then panic registered on his face. "I do it wrong."

"Hey, that's okay."

"I make a mistake." Riley's face started to scrunch up.

"Mistakes are okay," Kit soothed.

"Hey," West said, "It's a practice round."

The statement seemed to take Riley off guard. "What?"

"Practice. Mistakes don't count when you do a practice round. 'Cause it's the first time," West said. "It's your turn. Ask me for cards."

"I want cards please," the child said with careful, imitated intonation.

Kit wrapped an arm around Riley and whispered, "Ask do you

have any threes."

"Do you have any threes?" Riley echoed.

West fished out his three and handed it over.

AT TWO, Kit and Riley curled up together on the couch for a nap. West took the opportunity to get in touch with Evie and ask her if she knew anything about undoing a deal with a demon.

She told him she'd heard of it being done but didn't know how. She then offered to poke around to see what she could turn up. She also asked him if everything was alright and he told her he was asking for a friend, which sounded as untrue as it ever did.

He headed upstairs and combed through Laurel's room, looking for the grimoire. He should have felt bad, but he was just irritated when he couldn't find it.

When he returned downstairs, he found Kit in the kitchen, going through the cabinets, and Riley cocooned in blankets, still asleep on the couch.

"You need something?" West came to next to him and leaned against the counter.

Kit shot him a look.

"I mean, something tangible," West clarified.

"I don't know."

West hooked an arm around Kit's waist and tugged him close; he thought the demon would resist, but Kit pressed close, burying his face in West's shoulder. He let out a small keening sound, then pulled back, viciously rubbing his eyes.

"Hey," West said.

Kit shook his head. "No, it's fine, I'm fine."

"You're not. Come here."

"I—"

"Kit, come here, let me give you a hug," West insisted. He took his hands and tried to pull him back.

Kit yanked his hands back and snapped, "I don't need a *hug*, I need to fix this."

"You're such a *liar*," West told him, not able to keep a smile off his face.

"Stop trying to be cute."

West rolled his eyes, moved in a few steps, and threw his arms around Kit. The demon stepped back but West didn't let him go. "Stop fighting it."

"West, cut it out," Kit grumbled, putting his hands on West's chest and trying to weasel out of his grip.

West tightened his arms.

"Oh my god, you're really strong," Kit grunted.

"They didn't tell you that about witches?"

Kit stopped struggling. "Tell me what?"

West tightened his arms, pulling Kit in closer. He slid his arms down a little lower and lifted the demon off his feet. "Proportional strength of an ant."

Kit stiffened up. "That...there's no way that's true."

Being lifted wasn't anything that should have surprised Kit and West had to assume that no one had ever picked him up. Or maybe it was West's frame; he was slimmer than Kit and must have seemed scrawny in comparison to Mike. Maybe Kit was used to being hoisted around only by mountainous men covered with body hair.

"Of course not, it's called working out, you dork." West hoisted him higher and threw the demon over his shoulder.

"Alright, fine, color me impressed. Put me down."

With a little bit of maneuvering, West set Kit down on the counter. He rested his hands on the demon's thighs, one finger working its way inside one of the rips in Kit's jeans. He took the chance to appreciate the warmth of Kit's skin.

"Hey," Kit warned, his voice husky.

"What?"

"Riley—"

"Is asleep and I'm not even doing anything," West pointed out.

"You're doing something."

West offered, "We could do a lot more if you think he'll stay asleep."

Kit licked his lips, sucked in his bottom lip, and dug is teeth into it. Without waiting for an answer, West pushed between his legs and kissed him. He settled his hands on Kit's hips, dragging him closer. Kit raked his hands through West's hair and tilted his head back, his mouth roaming down West's jaw and throat.

West moaned, pulling Kit off the counter, needing to press himself against something more than the hard edge of the kitchen counter. Kit thrust against him and West started to fumble with the other man's jeans.

Kit caught his hands and pushed them back. "Not here."

"We can go downstairs," West offered.

Kit nodded, giving West a push towards the basement stairs. On the way, he glanced at Riley, then hesitated.

"He's asleep," West whispered. "Out like a light." He gave Kit a tug and when the demon still hesitated, West slipped his hand between his legs, caressing him.

Kit followed him after that, both of them rushing down the stairs. Once they both had their feet firmly on the ground again, West tugged off Kit's shirt and returned to kissing him; he let his mouth wander, sometimes sucking at his throat or tracing his tongue over the lines of Kit's tattoos.

Kit let out a shuddering breath and pushed West towards the bed. It was more than pushing, it was more like a shove and something about being handled like that dredged up a heat that West hadn't felt before.

Something like fear and anticipation molding together, making his breath come faster and his blood pound through his veins.

He expected Kit to climb on top of him, which he did, pushing between West's thighs, and he expected the speed with which they stripped each other of their clothing. He expected all of it, the scraping bites, wandering hands, and hungry kisses, until Kit straddled him. Kit leaned in to kiss him again before he straightened up.

His hand slid over West for a moment longer, then he took West inside of him with a sharp gasp followed by a long moan. The demon planted one hand firmly on West's chest and rocked his hips, slowly but then quickening, moving back and forth with a fervor West hadn't anticipated.

Being the conduit for another's pleasure wasn't unfamiliar to West but doing it in quite this way was. To lie beneath Kit, watching him roll and grind his way towards climax, was something West hadn't done with a man before. Watching him like this, seeing him undone and unguarded, did more for West than anything else ever had.

Afterward, when Kit tried to move away, West wrapped his arms around him and drew him close. He nuzzled his face against the other man's throat and kissed his shoulder. Kit remained stiff, awkwardly lying on his side as West tried to snuggle.

"What's wrong?" West asked.

"Nothing. What do you want?" the demon asked.

"Nothing, stupid, I just like being near you."

"Not going to kick me out again?"

Ah, so that was it, that was why he'd tensed up and looked so uncertain. West gave him another kiss. "Never."

"Promise?"

Usually, West didn't bother making promises to people and never bothered making them at all after sex, knowing how infrequently they were made with any intention to keep them. This time, though, he said, "I promise," and meant it.

Kit relaxed after that, melting into West's arms. West started to wonder how long it would be before he didn't feel like shit for kicking him out in the first place; he imagined them years in the future, laughing about it instead. The idea took him off guard. He hadn't thought about his future, especially not one with another person in it, for a while.

"I think I need to call my mom," West announced after a long contemplation of Kit's tattoos.

"Um."

West clarified, "About Riley. About the demon. She might...well, she might be more reasonable about helping than Laurel, at any rate. And she might have an idea of where to start."

"About this whole getting kicked out thing," Kit began.

"I'm a big boy, I can figure things out," West said, not sure that he wanted to hear whatever Kit might offer him.

"I can help you find a place if you want," he offered. "I, uh, weirdly enough, I know a bunch of real estate agents."

It wasn't the offer West had dreaded. "Yeah. Yeah, actually, that sounds perfect." He kissed Kit's cheek, then rolled out of bed. "Come on, we've got shit to do."

Upstairs, they found Riley still asleep.

West dug around for his phone and went out on the porch to

call his mother, sure that her voice would be loud enough for Kit to hear. Whatever she was going to have to say, it wouldn't be pretty.

He meant to be calm and straight forward about what had happened, but as soon as he heard her voice, the first thing that came out of his mouth was, "Mom, I need help."

"Where are you?"

"I'm at home."

"I'll be right over," she said and hung up.

He waited on the porch; after a few minutes, Kit poked his head out. "That didn't sound disastrous."

"I haven't told her anything yet."

Kit sat beside him and took out a cigarette. "Do you mind?" he asked, guilt scrawled across his face.

Thinking of what he had to tell his mother, lung cancer was the least of West's worries. "Go ahead."

"I know it's a bad habit," the demon admitted halfway through his cigarette. He flicked a bit of ash off and West had to admit, he looked cool.

"You should get a vape," West suggested just to see what the demon would do.

Kit gagged. He took a drag, then another. "It's gonna be bad, whatever your mom has to say?"

"Probably."

Kit nodded, his face drawn tight.

"If...listen. If she gets out of line or anything...just, you should know that it's not how I feel. Whatever she says," West told him.

The demon did nothing more than raise his eyebrows and press his lips together.

West gave the other man's hand a squeeze, knowing well there was nothing he could do to ease the sting.

By the time West's mother arrived, Riley had come out to join them on the porch. He'd settled onto his father's lap, asking when they could go home. Kit rolled an unlit cigarette between his fingers the whole time but didn't once put it to his lips.

Diana came up the front walk and looked them over, her eyes lingering on Kit and Riley as she said to West, "You know your sister told me you were mixed up with something bad."

"We're dating," West said and once he started, he couldn't stop blabbering, "I stole grandma's grimoire, Laurel's kicking me out, and when I was thirteen I made a deal with the Devil so Jeremey Nivens could keep playing baseball."

Kit stared at him and so did his mother.

"Start at the beginning," his mother said.

He did, at the very start, and told her about all the people who'd come to ask him questions, about what Kit had come to him about, up to the recent revelation about what Mike had done in his desperation to have the version of his son that he'd wanted. Explaining that part had involved a lot of mincing of words and guilty looks in Riley's direction.

The boy might have been young, and he certainly looked like he was off in his own world, but a frank discussion about how his father had wanted to fundamentally alter him would leave some kind of mark on his psyche.

When he'd finished explaining everything as best he could, West had the same feeling he did right after he'd drunk too much and thrown everything up.

His mother sighed and said to Kit, "You might as well give me one of those."

Kit handed over the cigarette he'd been fiddling with and lit it for her with a lick of conjured flame.

"Mom..."

She took a drag and let out the smoke through her nose. She continued to look at Kit. "We're gonna need to do an exorcism."

Kit nodded.

She held out one glittering hand to him. "Diana, by the way. Kit, was it?"

He shook her hand. "Clarence," he corrected then looked unsure as to why he'd done so. "But, uh, people call me Kit."

She walked past both of them. "Might as well get all this started. Westley, call your sister, we need that book."

They followed her in.

She glanced back at them. "When this is all taken care of, we're gonna have a talk about the two of you. Don't think we're not."

"Mom, it's not—"

"It's not what?" she asked. "Not something you hid from me? Not something you stole from me over?"

"It's not like that," West huffed. "I knew you wouldn't let me have the grimoire."

"How could you know that?"

He ignored the question. "And you were weird about knowing I even *worked* with demons."

She jabbed her finger towards him. "And this deal with the

Devil business, Westley! That's another thing. *That* we're going to talk about."

West opened his mouth to argue and thought better of it. Right now, they had to get this business with Riley fixed; anything his mother might have to say about Kit was just annoying compared to the idea of some monster doing who knew what to the child.

LAUREL HANDED over the grimoire but not without a stink. When their mother finally snapped at her, she fetched it and tossed it onto the kitchen table. Then she grabbed her purse and made for the door.

"Where are you going?" their mother asked.

"I'm not getting mixed up in this," Laurel answered with a sneer.

"You're going to put this boy in danger?" Diana asked. "We need someone else for this spell."

"I can't believe *he's* not what you're worried about," Laurel said, her eyes stabbing towards Kit.

West peeked at the spell. "We only need three. Kit can sub in for a witch, we did it before."

"We need four," Diana told him. "Three for the spell and one...Well." She looked at Kit. "One to keep the other creature distracted. This sort of thing goes easier if we don't have Hell-born things showing up to stop it."

Kit nodded, resigned to his position. He had his hands shoved into his pockets but West had seen them shaking before he'd hidden them. He hadn't said more than a few terse words since Laurel and his mother had started bickering.

To West's horror, Diana ripped out a page from the grimoire. She handed it over to the demon. "This is the spell you'll need to summon her. Best if you do it somewhere else, too. As long as you're talking with her, she won't be able to interrupt us."

Kit nodded again, staring down at the page. His eyes darted over the words, his lips moving.

Riley twirled and hopped around in the living room. West had shown him how to work their Bluetooth speaker and the boy hadn't stopped dancing since. It had bought them the time they needed to discuss everything without giving the poor kid nightmares.

Though he was about to be exorcized; if anything was going to give someone nightmares, it might be that.

West skimmed the ritual again, looking over what the spell required. Nothing abjectly horrifying jumped out, but then again, Riley was only four.

Not even old enough for kindergarten and he'd be slathered in herb paste and circled by witches chanting in an unknown language for the length of the spell. It would be tough for an adult to tolerate it without a bit of fidgeting or whining, without getting nervous.

And Riley hadn't stopped dancing for twenty minutes.

Kit stared into the living room, watching his son with a drawn look on his face.

"Are you ready?" Diana asked, her voice low and gentle.

Kit nodded. "Rye."

The boy ignored him.

"Riley!"

This time he looked.

"All done, turn it off," Kit told him.

Riley shook his head.

"Yes, all done. We have to do something else now. You can listen to music later." Kit went into the living room and turned off the speaker.

Riley didn't shriek or hit his father but started to cry as if his little heart had been broken. His hand balled into a fist and slammed into the side of his head.

Kit grabbed his wrist and pulled him in close. "Hey, Rye, hey, first this, then music. You're okay. You are."

The boy squirmed in his father's arms, screaming and kicking.

"Shhh, Rye, alright, come on, count to ten."

Riley didn't count to ten; if he heard his father's voice over his own cries, it would have been a miracle. He tried again to hit himself but Kit kept his arms firmly around the boy as he writhed and sobbed.

West watched as Kit tried to soothe his son. He bolted into the basement, grabbed what he needed, then came back upstairs.

"Give me the page," he demanded of Kit, who still cradled Riley close to his chest. The boy had stopped twisting but continued crying.

"What?"

"You don't know shit about demons," West told him, "I mean...not these ones. I've done this before and I know the rules. And I have something to trade."

"West," his mother warned.

West turned to face her. "No, Mom, just...Kit can stand in for me and he should be *here*."

"You're not making—"

"Mom! Would you ever have left me alone for something like this? The kid should be with his dad and Kit shouldn't be out there tangling with something he doesn't know anything about. The last guy who made a deal with this demon ended up dead." Before she could argue, West turned back to Kit. "Give me the page, alright?"

Over Riley's sniffling, exhausted tears, Kit said, "West, you don't have to..."

"Nobody has to do anything, Kit, now give me the fucking page." He stuck out his hand. "Please."

Kit took the page out of the back pocket and handed it over.

"Text me when he's ready."

Kit nodded.

West jogged out the front door, following his normal morning route to the halfway point. Two and a half miles should be far enough.

He fished the chalk out of his pocket and traced a circle onto the parking lot of a vet's office. He paced around the circle waiting for the go-ahead from Kit.

Once he got it, he sucked in a breath, smoothed out the pages, and began to chant. If he could summon the Devil for a no one like Jeremey Nivens then he could do this for Kit.

Rithys, short, stocky, and dark-haired, appeared in the center of the circle. Instead of human eyes, though, she had at least a half-dozen shiny black ones scattered across the top half of her face.

She looked around then looked him over. "Your pet is ill?" When she spoke, he glimpsed something behind her lips that resembled a spider's mouthparts.

"Uh. No." He looked around and realized the location might

have misled her. "I... Michael McAuliffe, you gave him this." He held up the suncatcher. "And you made a deal with him about his son. And, uh, you killed him."

"He reneged on his half," she informed his casually. Her many eyes scanned over the area, over West. "What of it, witchboy?"

"Yeah, well, people think his ex-husband had something to do with it."

Her head tilted to the side. "You...wish me to turn myself in to human authorities?" she guessed, genuinely puzzled.

"I want you to pin it on someone else. Some shit-sucking scumbag," West said.

"And in return?"

He fished around in the pocket of his jeans and took out a wooden coin. "This is good for—"

All six of her eyes oriented towards the coin in his hand. "I know what that is good for."

"You want it?"

"It will..." Her eyes narrowed and she bared her teeth. The things inside her mouth rubbed together. "It will suffice, the deal is made."

It had gone too fast. The spell the others needed to work would last for a while longer.

West stepped away from the circle, his mind scrabbling for ideas. "There's something else."

"I must go."

"We're still negotiating, Rithys," he reminded. "I haven't agreed to anything yet."

She chittered. "You're working with them."

He nodded. "Yeah. I am."

"The boy is *marked*."

"It was a bad deal, anyway. Why are you still holding out on your end?" he asked.

"The human reneged. That doesn't mean I didn't take what I was owed," she explained.

West wanted to ask what she had taken from Mike but decided against it. If he didn't know, he could never tell Kit; he didn't think the other man needed to know any more unsavory details about Mike's ill-fated adventures in making deals.

Rithys gurgled and asked, "What are the rest of your terms?"

West paced around the circle. "You deal in broken things. The kid's not broken."

"It's not for me to say what's broken or isn't. The rest of your terms!" the demon demanded.

West looked her over. Classing her and Kit both as demons had been a massive oversight. Of course, the terminology regarding Satan's children as demons had come about in the Low Middle Ages and they hadn't even had forks then. "What will you give me? To be done here?"

"What do you want? Anything you want you can have," Rithys offered, though her tone carried a hint of threat and panic.

"Money?"

"Yes," she snapped.

He could sense the irritation rolling off her, even when he cast his eyes towards the ground. "Power?"

"Of course."

"To eat as much as I want without getting fat?" he asked.

Rithys snarled, "What part of anything—"

"What about not caring if I get fat? Can you do that?"

The demon screeched and lunged for him.

The circle held but West jumped back anyway. He didn't know how long a circle like this would hold for or how long the exorcism would actually take. It would have been smart to ask before he'd gone running out the door.

Though this was almost preferable to having Laurel glower and snap at him.

"How about a job? A nice apartment?"

She didn't answer and reached for him again. She chittered and hissed when the circle zapped her. "As soon as this deal is over, I'm going to eat your guts."

"I don't think so."

"Do you know—"

"I work for your king," he told her.

The demon threw back her head and screamed, a low guttural sound. The things in her mouth spilled out and West thought he saw more limbs budding from her sides. She threw herself at the circle and it held, but it also flickered briefly.

His phone buzzed and his hand trembled as he drew it out of his pocket.

Kit telling him that spell was done.

West took out another coin. He held them both up. "One to get the blame off Kit; put it on some...child molester or something. One to never come near me or Kit or Riley ever again. Deal?"

She snarled and seethed, but she growled, "Deal."

He tossed the coins into the circle and stepped back. He flipped the page over and read the chant to dismiss her.

When he'd summoned the Devil, the beast had gone on his own, but West didn't trust Rithys not to pull his guts out through his nose, no matter what deal they'd struck.

He ran home, feeling like he was being followed, afraid to look back. He had never minded spiders before, but he didn't think he'd ever look at them the same way again.

He found Kit on the porch with Riley on his hip. The boy didn't have marks on his skin anymore, but he had circles under his eyes. Someone had found him a pair of headphones and West could make out the faint sound of John Denver music coming through.

Kit stood as West approached.

"I've got to get him home," Kit said. "But I wanted to say thanks."

"Sure. Poor guy had a tough day."

Kit looked at his boots.

Riley, his cheek against his father's chest, looked at West. Their eyes met for a second and West gave a wave.

Riley weakly returned the gesture then nestled closer against his father. Kit kissed his son's hair.

"Was it bad?" West asked.

"It wasn't good."

"At least it's done," West offered hopefully.

"Mm."

"Did my mom give you a hard time?"

The demon shook his head. "No, I think Rye put her off a little. Just that he exists not, you know, any of the other stuff."

Kit came down a step and West came up one, meeting him halfway. He put a hand on the demon's arm. "You want to meet up tomorrow maybe? We can talk about things."

Kit nodded. "Yeah. Uh. Thank you."

"If you really want to say thank you, you'll send me another one of those little hand-painted cards of yours."

The demon cracked a smile, then looped his free arm around West's shoulders. He pulled him in close and held him like that for a long time, his face nestled against the crook of West's neck.

When Kit stepped back, pulling in a long breath, West used his sleeve to dab the tears off the demon's cheeks and gave him a kiss.

"Call me," West told him. "Later. If you want to talk."

"I will." Kit scrubbed at his face with the heel of his hand. "Good luck with the two of them."

West shrugged and, hoping he sounded less worried than he was, said, "Ah, I just summoned a demon, what's the worst *they* can do to do me?"

"Listen, I'd get it if—"

"Don't be stupid. I'll see you tomorrow," West cut him off, not wanting to give the idea a moment's consideration. "Right?"

His chest tightened waiting for the answer; he didn't know what he would do if this had been too much, if Kit didn't want to see him anymore.

"Yeah." Kit headed down the steps.

"Hey," West called.

Kit glanced back. "What?"

"I meant it about the card."

Kit shifted Riley's weight. "I'll hand-deliver it."

West couldn't help skipping back down the steps to give him another kiss. He touched his forehead to Kit's and wanted to say something meaningful. "I can call you my boyfriend, right?"

Kit let out a small chuckle. "Yes."

They exchanged one more small kiss and Riley started to squirm.

West headed inside and sat through the barrage of questions and admonishments that his mother and sister threw at him.

"Were you ever even going to *tell us* that you were dating a demon?" his mother asked.

"You know he wasn't," Laurel huffed and glared at him. "Which means he knows it's a *stupid idea*."

"How long has this been going on?"

He tuned them out and spent most of the lecture time combing through his phone to find pictures of him and Kit together. He'd taken a handful over the past few weeks and once he'd stitched them together the way he wanted, it took him even longer to try to come up with the right hashtags.

"West, are you listening?" his mother demanded, pushing his phone away.

He looked up. "Yeah, I know, lying's wrong. Can you blame me, though? Being honest got me kicked out," he said with a glance towards Laurel.

"And that's another thing," his mother began, turning to face her daughter. "You're not kicking your brother out."

"He's not staying here, not if he's going have that *creature–!*"

"First, he has a fucking name," West snapped instinctively. "And second, I don't want to stay here if you're going to be a bitch about it. I'll be gone on Friday, just like you said."

"Friday! Laurel!" his mother cried and really started to lay into his sister for kicking him out.

West never settled on a hashtag and put the pictures up anyway. He did successfully find Kit's barely used handful of social media profiles and tag him in the pictures. He didn't know what any of Kit's friends would think of it, or even if he had many friends. He didn't know what his own friends would think. Maybe they'd be happy for him.

He'd worry about what other people thought once he could get the image of those *things* inside Rithys' mouth out of his head.

Or maybe he wouldn't worry about what other people thought at all. He let the continued arguing from his mother and sister wash over him for a while longer. He stood up, stretched, and announced, "I'm going to bed."

They looked at him.

"West, we're worried about you," his sister insisted.

He shrugged. "I'm gonna go pack a fucking bowl and get some sleep. In the morning, I'm gonna help my boyfriend process some of his trauma, and then I'm gonna figure out not being homeless and unemployed before Friday. So you can keep your worry to yourself."

He walked out of the kitchen.

"Westley," his mother said.

He had to stop and look at her, the tone in her voice left no room for anything else. "Mom."

"You're going to come stay with me until you get this figured out."

He sighed.

She came over to him and took his hands. "I've worried about you a lot, West. You've been in a tough place for a while. But tonight you did something good for that boy and his father."

"I really like him, Mom."

She squeezed his hands. "You acted with more purpose than you have in years. If he can do that for you..." She sighed. "We'll see where this goes."

West swallowed. She hadn't accepted anything yet, but she'd

opened herself to the possibility.

"Get some sleep. Start packing. Your room is just how you left it."

"The idea of sleeping in a twin bed with poster of Channing Tatum above it is not the most appealing thing I've heard."

"Don't be fresh." She hugged him.

He hugged her back for a long time. How long had it been since he'd hugged his mother like this? Since he'd even talked about anything meaningful with her? "I love you, Mom."

"I love you too, baby."

He retreated to the basement and slept soundly. Maybe it was the pot, but maybe it was the feeling that, for the first time in a while, he actually knew what he wanted.

About the Author

Dan is an author and educator who has lived in Connecticut for their entire life. They received a degree in education and later wrote their Master's thesis on representation of women in same-sex relationships in contemporary Spanish literature and cinema.

What Everyone Deserves
2017 Rainbow Awards **Honorable Mention**
"Although the story deal with some real 1950's issues – discrimination, homophobia, interracial couples and hate crimes – it did it in a way that perfectly suited the characters and the story." - Divine Magazine

In this 1950s period drama, Junius is a New York City fertility demon with a crush. Ever since falling from heaven he's been alone. Except for the mothers and children he watches over.

James Kelly Rosenburg, a black soldier with snowflakes in his hair, walks right into his life with a big problem. James Kelly, turned vampire during the war, is new to New York and its prohibition against vampire killing in city limits.

Junius offers to teach him to overcome his bloodthirsty instincts and live a proper Manhattan life. Their growing friendship leaves them both conflicted as they explore a city both welcoming and alienated by their kind.

That Doesn't Belong Here
"I liked the ... atmosphere that he created, alongside the paranormal creatures that roam the street. I liked that he wrote characters I could emotionally care for. If Ackerman writes another LGBT fiction, I will give it a try for sure." - Ami, **The Blogger Girls**

That Doesn't Belong Here begins when Levi and his friend Emily discover an impossible creature in an abandoned pick up. The thing is wounded, frightened and the two friends cannot leave him to the mercy of rubberneckers and tourists. This novel explores what it means to be a person, as the creature, Kato, begins to display not mere intelligence or friendliness but what can only be explained as humanity. The question of who we are allowed to love arises for Levi and Kato, as they are not just crossing the boundaries of gender or sexuality, but of species.

www.ingramcontent.com/pod-product-compliance
Lightning Source LLC
Chambersburg PA
CBHW062309200726
48292CB00004BA/1462